Elizabeth Daleiden on Trial

A Novel By

I0566674

Ron Fritsch

Published by Asymmetric Worlds

For information, address:

Ron Fritsch
1657 West Winona Street
Chicago, IL 60640-2707

https://www.elizabethdaleiden.com

For David, Lee Ann and my family

The Characters
Listed Alphabetically by Their First Names

Albert Gartner, a former co-owner of a hardware store in Revere

Anna Bachman, Elizabeth's maternal grandmother, Karl's sister, Emma's mother

Belle Remington, Violet's partner, the owner of a bookstore in Oxford

Charlene Tillich, a court reporter

Clyde Lewis, a former deputy sheriff who testifies about the fire on December 17, 1955

Colby Smith, a former deputy sheriff who testifies about Jacob's death on May 25, 1950

Daniel Daleiden, Elizabeth's husband, Eli's father, Olivia's son

Darrell Glendenning, the Concord County sheriff in 1977, Warren's cousin, Royal's grandson

Eli Daleiden, Elizabeth and Daniel's only child, Olivia's grandson

Elizabeth Daleiden, Eli's mother, Daniel's wife, Emma and Jacob's daughter

Emma Bachman, Elizabeth's mother, Karl's niece, Anna's daughter, Jacob's wife

Eric Sorenson, Thane's brother, a former congressman

Frank Kerrigan, Jonah's former boyfriend, later his tenant

Gideon Heidecker, the judge who presides at Elizabeth's trial

Henry Hassenauer, Elizabeth's neighbor, Titus's partner, who dies on December 17, 1955

Jacob Reifert, Elizabeth's father, Emma's husband, who dies on May 25, 1950

Jill Foster, a Chicago television news reporter

Jonah Neumeyer, a twenty-eight-year-old lawyer and former neighbor of Elizabeth's

Karl Bachman, Elizabeth's great-uncle, Emma's uncle, Anna's brother

Mike Hammond, a friend of Frank's, Tom's partner

Olivia Daleiden, Elizabeth's mother-in-law, Daniel's mother, Eli's grandmother

Paul Sikorski, a lawyer who introduces Jonah to Thane

Royal Glendenning, the Concord County sheriff in the 1950s, Darrell and Warren's grandfather

Tanner Howland, the Concord County state's attorney in 1977

Thane Sorenson, an attorney who provides expert testimony in Elizabeth's trial

Titus Peltz, Elizabeth's neighbor, Henry's partner, who dies on December 17, 1955

Tom Cutler, a friend of Frank's, Mike's partner

Tony Marino, a hay buyer

Violet Sutherland, Elizabeth's attorney, Belle's partner

Warren Glendenning, Tanner's opponent for a congressional seat, Royal's grandson

Chapter One

Elizabeth Daleiden had to know, better than anybody else, what happened the night Henry and Titus died in the fire that destroyed their house. They were her nearest neighbors. They'd left her their farm, too.

Jonah Neumeyer felt he had no alternative but to go back to Revere to pay her a visit. He'd always imagined he'd start with Elizabeth.

He showed up at her farm at the time they'd agreed upon, which was two o'clock in the afternoon on the first Saturday in April 1977. It also happened to be the day Jonah turned twenty-eight.

After parking his car in her driveway, he walked to her back door, which was the door to her kitchen, and knocked. That was what farmers in Revere Township in Concord County in northern Illinois did when they visited one another.

He hadn't seen her for almost ten years, not since he graduated from high school and left Revere. As soon as she opened her door, he was pleased to see she was still, in her midforties, the Elizabeth Daleiden of his boyhood.

Five feet ten inches tall, the same as Jonah, she did the outdoor farmwork men did. Despite that strike against her, many of Jonah's male classmates in high school had agreed they'd gladly sacrifice one of their balls to end a date with her in the backseat of their car.

Without hesitating, she embraced Jonah, and he gladly returned her hug.

Unlike his classmates, he'd always wished she were his mother.

Releasing Jonah, but still holding his hands, Elizabeth looked him up and down.

As he did her.

They both wore plain white tee shirts, faded Levis and scuffed gym shoes. They both had light-brown hair with only a suggestion of a wave in it. They both had it cut too short for the times. He was without facial hair. She was without makeup.

Their eyes meeting again, they laughed.

Elizabeth spoke first. "I heard you did well in college and law school. You must've, to be where you are now."

Jonah worked for one of the largest firms in Chicago. They'd hired him out of law school three years ago. Less than six months later, the group of lawyers handling matters for the firm's bank client asked him to work full time with them. He promptly, happily accepted their offer. It put him on a certain path to a partnership—if he behaved himself.

Elizabeth offered him a seat at her kitchen table and asked if he'd like coffee.

"Yes, thank you," he replied, sitting down. "Black, please."

"That's the way I like it, too. As black as Concord County topsoil."

After handing him a cup on a saucer, she sat down at the table with her own.

Jonah told her he was "awfully saddened" when he learned her husband died the day after last Christmas.

"Daniel was in a great deal of pain," Elizabeth said. "The doctors told us there was nothing more they could do. The cancer had spread throughout his body."

"I heard that. I'm very sorry. I have to confess, when I was growing up out here, I admired Daniel Daleiden. Maybe your being his wife had a lot to do with that."

Elizabeth smiled. "You were the boy who fired your grandmother's hired man."

Jonah smiled back. "I was that boy."

Elizabeth wasn't about to stop there. "How old were you when you did that?"

"Thirteen."

"People said you told your grandmother you'd do the hired man's work yourself, and she wouldn't have to pay you."

Jonah knew how he was remembered in Revere. He was the strange boy who not only fired his grandmother's hired man and did the work himself. He also cared for his grandmother during what the neighbors referred to as her "declining years," while he was in high school.

His teachers readily excused him from classes on days he called to explain he had farmwork to do or his grandmother had taken a turn for the worse. They knew he was telling the truth. They also knew he'd rather be in school, arguing with them and his classmates about whatever it was they were attempting to teach and learn that day. He likewise knew his teachers were telling the truth when they said they'd miss him.

"Something happened when I was six years old," Jonah said, "and it's bothered me ever since. I think you're probably the one person in the world who can help me understand what I saw and heard that night."

Without taking her eyes off Jonah's, Elizabeth nodded.

"Henry and Titus and the fire," she said.

Without taking his eyes off Elizabeth's, Jonah also nodded.

"That night," he said.

*****

One December evening in 1955, which the weatherman on television had correctly predicted would be "bitterly cold," Jonah and his grandmother watched a fire consume a farmhouse down the road from theirs. Two elderly men, Henry and Titus, lived in it. They'd claimed to be brothers.

"I still dream about it," Jonah told Elizabeth. "And it's just as frightening in my dreams now as it was when it happened."

"I remember you were there with your grandmother. I was worried about you and what you saw. Children shouldn't see such things. I can understand why you'd still dream about it."

"I wish I'd come to speak with you about this earlier," Jonah said. "I can only admit I've lacked the courage to do it—to find out the truth."

The volunteer firemen from Revere and two neighboring townships arrived in their ancient fire trucks and struggled with freezing hoses. Elizabeth and her husband Daniel, both twenty-three, were two of the youngest firemen. The fire burnt most of the house to the ground. It also burnt "beyond recognition," as the *Oxford Times* reported, the two men who lived there.

The firemen and deputy sheriffs covered the men's bodies with tarpaulins before they brought them out on stretchers.

"Who set fire to their house?" Jonah asked Elizabeth. "Do you know?"

"The sheriff and the coroner said it must've been an accident.

3

I'm certain that's what it was. Henry was eighty-five. Titus was seventy-five. They were in poor health."

"Did you know they weren't brothers?" Jonah asked.

Elizabeth glanced at Jonah's left hand. He wasn't wearing a ring. She probably would've heard about it if he had any reason to be wearing one.

"I knew they weren't brothers," she said. "Hassenauer was Henry's last name. They told people that was Titus's last name, too, but it wasn't. His was Peltz. They got away with it for a long time. I knew what they were doing."

"Do you know why they passed themselves off as brothers?" Jonah asked.

"I think you know why they did that."

"I can only guess," Jonah said. "But my guess is they didn't want people to know they were gay."

Elizabeth smiled. "I never heard them use that word to describe themselves. I would've remembered it if I had. But if that's what you wish to call them now, then that's what they were—two gay men living together, sleeping in the same bed. I was often in their house."

Jonah hadn't expected Elizabeth to go that far.

Jonah pointed at a kitchen window facing west.

"Wasn't that their barn?"

"Yes, it was. We still use it."

"And their house was about halfway between their barn and the road?"

"Yes."

"So it wasn't far from where we're sitting now," Jonah said. "You and Daniel might've seen people sneaking into it to set it on fire."

Elizabeth emptied her cup and placed it on the saucer in front of her.

"Daniel and I undoubtedly would've seen people entering the house the night it burned," she said. "We could see both their back and front doors from all our west-facing windows. They had their porch lights on. They always did when it was dark. But we didn't see anybody sneak into their house that night. We didn't see anybody near the house until the fire started. The fire was what the officials said it was: a dreadful accident."

4

"Didn't that house have windows on its other side, facing west?"

"Yes, of course. Several windows."

"What if the intruder, or intruders, knew the men? They would've also known you and Daniel could see both of their doors. Wouldn't they choose to sneak into the house through a window on the west side of it?"

Elizabeth stared at Jonah.

"Nobody sneaked into their house that night," she said. "Not through any of their doors or windows."

"Were you in the house when the fire started?"

"No, of course not. As soon as we saw it, Daniel and I ran over there and tried to put it out ourselves. Just the two of us, though, couldn't make a difference."

"But if you weren't in the house when the fire started, how do you know intruders didn't set it? How can you be certain of such a thing?"

"I know what you want me to tell you, Jonah. You want me to say people from around here paid Henry and Titus a visit after they learned the men weren't really brothers. And that visit—or 'intrusion,' as you might call it—led to the fire and the deaths of Henry and Titus."

"I'll never forget," Jonah said, "what I heard one man say when the firemen and deputies brought out their bodies: 'Those two old queers got what they deserved.' Then he asked: 'Who do we thank for setting their house on fire?'"

Elizabeth winced. "Daniel and I heard the horrible things some of the people said that night, after they knew Henry and Titus were dead. But their remarks don't mean anybody actually set the fire. I'm certain it was an accident and nothing else. Maybe it was an accident those nasty people welcomed, but they didn't set it."

"I don't know how you can be so sure no intruder, or intruders, set the fire. You said the people around here had just found out Henry and Titus weren't brothers."

Elizabeth chose to remain silent.

"No," Jonah pushed on, "the two old men weren't brothers after all. I heard what people were saying that night. Henry and Titus had turned out to be 'faggots.'"

Elizabeth cringed.

5

"I'm sorry," Jonah said.

Elizabeth shook her head. "No. You have no reason to be sorry. That was a word some ignorant people used to describe Henry and Titus."

Jonah remained silent.

Elizabeth had the prominent cheekbones, nose and chin of Nefertiti, a face that might've seemed gaunt and unforgiving were it not for the lips Daniel must've found bliss to meet with his.

"I hope you understand something," she said. "I would've gone over there and saved Henry and Titus myself. I would've shielded them from the people you think attacked them. Nobody would've dared touch them. Those two men were my dearest friends. I loved them. Everybody knew that. You knew that."

"I did," Jonah said. "And that's why I had to come to talk with you."

"And I'm glad you did," Elizabeth said. "I can see why you might believe a crowd of loudmouths murdered Henry and Titus. But I can guarantee you nothing like that happened."

*****

As Jonah said good-by to Elizabeth at her back door later that afternoon, he pointed toward a sunlit field across the blacktop road that ran past her house.

Somebody dressed like them in a white tee shirt and Levi's was driving a tractor pulling a manure spreader over the previous year's corn stalks, preparing the field for planting.

"Your son?" Jonah asked.

"Yes," Elizabeth replied. "That's Eli."

Eli had the front-end loader attached to the tractor. He'd used that back at the barn to dig into the hog manure and straw bedding and dump the mixture into the spreader. He'd probably also wielded a pitchfork to load what the machine missed.

Jonah could see Elizabeth and Eli were farming the same way he and his grandmother had farmed in the Fifties and Sixties.

"He's eighteen now," Elizabeth said. "He's still in high school, but he'll graduate next month. He reminds me of you. He enjoys

6

working. Farmwork, schoolwork, any kind of work. Whatever he does, he keeps at it until it's done."

She looked across the field at Eli, Jonah thought, as if she were an adoring Mary in a medieval painting.

Chapter Two

The next Thursday afternoon Jonah received a telephone call at work from a person who told the receptionist she was "Olivia Daleiden, the late Daniel Daleiden's mother." Olivia wished to speak with Jonah in person.

He agreed to meet her after work that day at his place.

*****

Jonah owned a two-flat in Lincoln Park. He'd bought it run-down and cheap when he went to work for the law firm in 1974. He paid a contractor to fix it up.

Frank Kerrigan was the man Jonah shared a dormitory room with at the University of Illinois at Champaign-Urbana during most of college and all of law school. Frank became his second-floor tenant. Jonah lived in the first-floor apartment. They both tended the backyard garden, attempting to outdo one another with their roses, lilies and phlox.

Frank's grades in law school weren't as good as Jonah's. He went to work for a small firm in the Loop collecting debts. Some of their classmates who worked in legal assistance offices representing people who couldn't afford lawyers chided Frank for "working for the bad guys." Those were the companies that financed the purchase of useless used cars, shoddy home repairs and worthless trade school diplomas.

"And that huge goddamned bank client you spend so many hours toiling away for," Frank liked to remind Jonah, "profits from the loans it makes to the bad guys I represent."

Frank also told Jonah he thought Elizabeth was lying.

"But why?" Jonah asked. "She knew those men were gay. She said she'd lay down her life for them. Nobody would dare attack them. You should've heard her go on."

Frank touched his gin gimlet glass to his lower lip.

"She's hiding something," he said.

*****

"You live here alone?" Olivia Daleiden asked Jonah after she took a seat on his couch and accepted a glass of his white wine.

"I live here alone," Jonah replied.

"I'll come right to the point, Mr. Neumeyer. My church held a birthday celebration for me on Sunday. I turned seventy-five the day before."

Jonah wasn't ready to tell Olivia they shared a birthday. He remembered who she was in Revere—the bank teller's wife, Daniel Daleiden's mother—but he couldn't recall previously speaking with her.

Olivia was like Elizabeth in one respect. She was still remarkably slender. Her heavy makeup, though, made her face look unreal, like a mannequin's. Jonah wondered if she thought it concealed her age.

"I suppose I should consider myself lucky," Olivia continued. "My one grandchild was brave enough to show up for the celebration."

"Eli?"

"Yes, Eli. I assume he did it because I'm his only living grandparent and he felt it was his duty. I'm quite certain he didn't do it because he feels any love for me. It's been a long time now since Elizabeth turned him against his paternal grandmother."

"Elizabeth didn't attend your party?"

Olivia scoffed. "Of course not. It was at St. Mary's, the Catholic church in Oxford."

Jonah remembered that, too. Daniel's family was Roman Catholic.

"In any event," Olivia continued, "Eli was telling the other guests that you'd paid his mother a visit the day before."

Jonah also recalled the rather modest house in Revere where the Daleidens lived. Daniel's father worked at the Revere State Bank for most of his life. Jonah had heard he died within a month after he retired at sixty-five. Like Eli, Daniel was an only child.

"Eli said you went to see his mother to talk about that awful fire."

"That was my purpose."

"He says you think a mob set the house on fire. After they found out the two old men weren't brothers."

Jonah set his wine glass down on the coffee table between him and his visitor.

"I don't have any doubt about it," he said. "It's obvious that's what happened."

"Does Elizabeth agree with you? Does she believe whoever murdered those old men should be brought to justice at long last?"

"No, she doesn't. She insists their deaths were an accident. She told me whenever it was as cold as it was that night, Henry and Titus burned wood in their living room fireplace. They didn't believe in spending money to buy a screen for protection from stray sparks. One must've popped out from the burning logs and started the fire that consumed the house. And the two men, who were elderly and ill, couldn't extinguish it before it got out of hand."

Olivia set her glass down on the coffee table.

"That's what Elizabeth says? That's the nonsense she talks?"

"I admit I don't understand what Elizabeth told me," Jonah said. "She insists only Henry and Titus were in the house when the fire started. But how could she know that if she wasn't there herself? She says, though, she wasn't."

"Mr. Neumeyer," Olivia said, "I know you're a big-city lawyer in a prestigious firm. But I don't think you see two things you ought to see."

"Two things I ought to see?" Jonah asked.

"Elizabeth's two lies."

Jonah remained silent.

"Believe me, she's quite capable of telling them."

Olivia smiled at Jonah. She could tell her blunt remarks had surprised him.

"Her first lie," she continued, "is her insisting those two old men weren't murdered. She knows that isn't true."

Jonah thought Olivia, picking up her glass again, looked rather pleased with herself.

"What's Elizabeth's second lie?" he asked.

Olivia was prepared for the question.

"Her saying she wasn't present in the house when the fire started."

*****

Elizabeth Daleiden's farm consisted of 320 acres, two quarter-sections lying side by side. A creek in a shallow valley ran through them both west to east, its water headed for the Fox, Illinois and Mississippi rivers.

She'd inherited the east quarter-section from her father, Jacob Reifert. He died in 1950 a few days before she graduated from Revere High School.

She and her classmate Daniel Daleiden had informed their parents they wished to marry that summer. Olivia and Daniel's father, as well as Elizabeth's father, refused to consent to the marriage. At eighteen, Elizabeth could marry without parental consent, but Daniel couldn't.

Elizabeth and Daniel therefore decided to live together unmarried. Three years from then, when they were twenty-one and Daniel no longer required parental consent, they'd marry.

Jacob Reifert left no will. Elizabeth took ownership of his 160-acre farm under the Illinois inheritance law. She was his only child. Her mother, his only spouse, had died when Elizabeth was five years old.

Daniel moved into Elizabeth's house the day they graduated from high school. They seemed not to care that, by living together as husband and wife without a legal marriage, they created what people told Jonah, growing up, was "one of the biggest scandals Revere has ever seen." And, his informants would add, their community had "more than its share" of those.

Elizabeth became the owner of the west quarter-section when Henry and Titus died the night of the fire in 1955. They'd made her a joint owner of their farm with what the legal papers referred to as the "right of survivorship."

Elizabeth deeded their farm to herself and her husband, Daniel. She'd done the same thing with her father's farm after she inherited it.

*****

In the fall of the year Jonah turned fourteen, after firing his grandmother's hired man and taking responsibility for her farm, he found himself in trouble. The forecasters were predicting a heavy rain that would turn to snow. Jonah didn't have nearly enough time to finish picking the corn before the rain was supposed to begin.

"*Mach schneller*," his grandmother told him in German. He had to hurry up.

Driving past the Neumeyer farm on their way home from grocery shopping in the town of Revere early one morning, Elizabeth and Daniel could see, just by looking at the fields, the predicament Jonah was in.

They drove their corn picker and two wagons to the Neumeyer farm that same morning. They assured Jonah they'd already finished their own corn harvest. They'd left Eli with a responsible neighbor who'd taken care of him before.

Elizabeth and Daniel spent two days helping Jonah pick the last of his grandmother's corn before the November storm began. The three of them worked so hard they had little time for conversation, but Elizabeth and Daniel did tell Jonah they admired him for firing his grandmother's hired man. If he needed any other help, all he had to do was call them.

Jonah knew only Elizabeth and Daniel kept him from losing most of his grandmother's corn that frightful autumn in 1963. But he promised himself they'd never have to do it again. What had he ever done to merit the astonishing kindness of Elizabeth and Daniel Daleiden?

Chapter Three

The third Saturday in April 1977 began with rain. The weather people predicted it would continue, on and off, into the evening.

Jonah had just finished putting his lunch dishes away when the bell rang.

As soon as he opened the front door, he knew his unexpected visitor could only be Daniel and Elizabeth Daleiden's eighteen-year-old son, taking the day off from the spring field work because of the rain.

And his visitor quickly confirmed who he was.

"I'm Eli Daleiden," he said.

"Please come in," Jonah said.

*****

Like Daniel, Eli was a couple inches taller than Jonah. Maybe twenty pounds heavier as well, all of it brawn. In a fight of any kind, friendly or otherwise, Jonah would've needed to use every trick he could think of to defeat him.

As his grandmother Olivia had done, Eli chose to take a seat on Jonah's leather couch.

He couldn't have been more than eight years old the last time Jonah saw him—the lucky boy who was Elizabeth and Daniel Daleiden's only child.

Eli took off his dark blue windbreaker and laid it on the couch next to him. His Levi's fit him as snugly as his Eagles tee shirt did.

Daniel and Eli had both inherited Olivia's dark brown hair and eyes. Eli was Nefertiti even more than Elizabeth was.

"Would you like something to drink?" Jonah asked. "Coffee?"

"No, thank you," Eli replied. "I didn't come here for pleasantries."

Jonah sat down in the chair he'd occupied during Olivia's visit.

Eli glared at him. "The purpose of my visit, asshole, is to let you know how much trouble you've stirred up."

"How much trouble I've stirred up?" Jonah asked.

"You seem to live in some kind of dreamworld here. My mother says you're a lawyer in a big Chicago firm. I assume I'm supposed to be impressed. I can see you live in a beautiful house. People must envy you. Then you come back to Revere, raising all sorts of questions and digging up the dead. I bet you don't have any idea the devastation you left behind."

"Devastation?" Jonah asked. "I'm sorry. I don't know what you're talking about."

"I knew you'd say that. I should've been there when you showed up. I should've kicked your ass out the door the minute you started pointing your goddamned finger at my mother. Although I don't imagine that would've stopped you from calling her a liar."

"I never called your mother a liar."

"Yes, you did. In so many words, you told my grandmother my mother was a liar. And my grandmother went straight to the state's attorney's office in Oxford. He agreed with her what you told her was important. Next thing you know, my mother has to hire a lawyer. And the state's attorney tells the lawyer—Violet Sutherland, maybe you know her—you'll get a subpoena to attend a grand jury hearing. The state's attorney wants you to testify about what my mother said to you when you saw her two weeks ago."

Oxford was the Concord County seat.

"The state's attorney," Jonah asked, with no little dread in his voice, "thinks he's found somebody to charge with murdering Henry and Titus?"

"Yeah, he does. And it'll be a high-publicity trial for him, thanks to you."

"Who does the state's attorney think murdered those men?"

"My mother."

*****

Jonah shook his head. "Your mother didn't murder Henry and Titus. That's crazy."

"Oh, and another thing," Eli said. "The state's attorney thinks my mother also murdered her father, my grandfather. He died twenty-seven years ago, in 1950. Violet says there's no statute of limitations for murder. But you'd know all about that."

"Why would your mother murder her father and her neighbors?"

"The state's attorney says her motives to commit those murders

16

are obvious."

Jonah stared at Eli. "To become the owner of their farms?"

"Bingo. To become the owner of the three-hundred-twenty-acre farm she and my father owned and worked for the last twenty-two years. The farm she and I live on today."

"This has gotten out of hand."

"Yeah, thanks to your meddling, it has."

*****

Jonah shook his head again. "I didn't go to see your mother to accuse her of anything. I thought she'd be the best person in the world to verify that a homophobic crowd murdered two gay men after finding out they weren't the brothers they claimed to be."

Eli stared back at Jonah across the coffee table. The rain had begun again.

"Of course," Jonah said, "an eighteen-year-old straight guy like yourself probably doesn't give a damn what happened to two old gay men in Revere back in 1955."

"Whether I'm straight or not," Eli said, "doesn't have anything to do with this."

That remark persuaded Jonah not to pursue the matter of his guest's sexual orientation any further.

Eli, though, was willing to speak openly about Jonah's.

"You live here by yourself?" he asked.

"A friend of mine from college and law school lives in the second-floor apartment."

"Is he your lover?"

"No."

"Do you have a lover?"

"No."

"Why not? You're a successful lawyer. You keep yourself in great shape. I wouldn't be surprised if gay guys were beating your door down and throwing themselves at your feet."

The first thing Jonah and Frank did after they moved into the two-flat was to put a home gym in the basement. They used it or ran along the lakefront every morning before they went to work.

They often ran together. Frank thought they got more attention that way.

"I'm sorry," Eli said. "Those questions were out of line. Your personal life is none of my business."

Jonah couldn't answer Eli's last question truthfully anyway. He'd have to tell him none of the men he'd met could compare with the man he fell in love with during his boyhood: Daniel Daleiden.

*****

"I don't understand," Jonah said, "how the state's attorney thinks he can get murder indictments based upon what your mother told me. I think I know why she insists no intruders could've set the house on fire. Henry and Titus were her friends. They left her their farm. They were old and in poor health. She saw herself as their protector. She doesn't want to admit some homophobes could've gotten into the house through a window on the side she and your father couldn't see. And after they were in the house, they could've killed the old men somehow and set the place on fire. She'd have to concede she failed her friends when they needed her the most."

"Violet, the lawyer, says the state's attorney has come up with some other evidence proving my mother did it."

"Other evidence? Against your mother?"

"You'll have to talk with Violet. And I hope you do it as soon as possible. The state's attorney thinks my mother was telling you the truth when she said there was no mob and there were no intruders. She told you the truth because she didn't want you to do what you did."

"What was it I did?"

"You called people's attention to an old crime, a crime my mother supposedly committed. That's what the state's attorney says she was trying to prevent. She failed, and now she's going to be indicted and put on trial for murder."

Jonah glanced at the rain streaking down the window behind Eli.

"But initially I only spoke with your mother," Jonah said, looking at Eli again. "I didn't call anybody else's attention to an old crime. You did that. You told people at your grandmother's birthday party about my visit. I spoke openly with your grandmother only because you didn't seem to care what she knew. Didn't you say she's the one who went to the state's attorney?"

"Okay, Jonah, I know. I'm in this with my big mouth just as much as you are with your meddling. I was so stupid. It was my grandmother's birthday party. She hates my mom. She always has. I could've stayed home. I didn't have to go."

"Your grandmother said you were brave to show up for her party."

"Thoughtless is a far better word than brave for what I did that day."

*****

"I hope you understand, Jonah. We're in this together. You and I opened the door, and the Concord County state's attorney is going to walk right through it. He's going to ask a grand jury to indict my mother for three murders. You know damned well she didn't kill her neighbors or her father."

"I'm quite certain your mother has never entertained the thought of committing murder."

"I don't know why the state's attorney thinks he can prove she killed her father. People who knew him said he was an alcoholic who drank whiskey for breakfast. One day she found him dead in his bed. And that didn't surprise anybody."

"That's what my grandmother told me," Jonah said. "Maybe the state's attorney wants potential jurors to think she's some kind of serial murderer. You know, she's secretly killing people despite her innocent appearance. And anybody could be her victim—if they have something she wants, like one hundred sixty acres of farmland."

The rain was letting up again.

"Look at this goddamned world," Jonah said. "For twenty-two years, the politicians who ran Concord County neglected the case of two gay men killed in their home by a mob. Then when one of those authorities finally decides to do something about it, he goes after the only person in the world who knew the men weren't brothers and loved them anyway."

"We're in this together," Eli said.

"You're damned right we are," Jonah said.

*****

"Violet told my mother if the jury convicts her, she'll go to prison for the rest of her life."

Jonah couldn't imagine Elizabeth Daleiden spending even one day in prison, let alone the rest of her life.

"My grandmother," Eli continued, "says my mother is damned lucky they can't give her what she really deserves."

Jonah could barely raise his voice above a whisper. "What's that?"

"The electric chair. The one they keep in that prison in Joliet."

Jonah felt unable to speak sensibly. How could anybody wish such a fate upon Elizabeth Daleiden?

"Violet says the courts have thrown out the death penalty for murders as old as the ones my mother supposedly committed."

Jonah knew that was true, but even life in prison was something he didn't wish to contemplate for Elizabeth.

"But Violet also told my mother she'll lose her farm if she's convicted."

Once again, Jonah stared at Eli, who seemed intent upon breaking his heart.

"It's called the Slayer Rule," Jonah said.

"What's that mean?"

"You can't inherit anything from people you murder. Your mother inherited her property from the three men the state's attorney says she murdered. Her lawyer is right. Your mother will also lose her farm. Both quarter-sections. Her whole damned farm."

*****

"I've got to go home," Eli said.

Jonah looked at his clock on the mantel above his fireplace. It was after four, almost three hours since his unexpected guest had begun their conversation by calling him an asshole.

"How'd you get here?" Jonah asked.

"I took the train. My mother drove me to the station in Oxford. She encouraged me to see you. She said I should've called you first, though. I found your address in a Chicago phone book the principal's secretary has at school. Some people on the train told me how to get here on the El. I could've taken a cab if I had to."

"I'll drive you home," Jonah said.

"You don't need to do that. I'll catch the next train. I'll call my mother from a pay phone in Union Station. All I have to do is let her know the arrival time for the train in Oxford."

Jonah shook his head.

"I admit," Eli said, "I've never come into Chicago on my own before. I could tell my mother was worried at first, when I let her know what I wanted to do. But then she told me to do it anyway. She said I should meet you. And you can see I got this far okay. I'm sure I can find my way home, too. You must have plans. It's a Saturday night."

Jonah shook his head again. "I did have plans, but I've decided to change them. Give me a few minutes to make a call or two."

Chapter Four

As soon as Frank got out of bed the next day, he came down to see Jonah, who was eating lunch and reading a book in his kitchen.

Frank found a clean cup, helped himself to Jonah's coffee and sat down at his table.

"My God," he said, "that one was cute. Young, too. Where did you find him?"

Jonah had seen Frank on his back deck looking down at him and Eli when they left the previous afternoon.

"Have you ever wondered," Jonah asked, "why your life is so superficial and empty you have to resort to spying on me for your amusement?"

Frank laughed.

"That cute young man," Jonah said, "wasn't somebody I picked up somewhere and brought home for sex."

"I'm sorry to hear that. Who was he? And why was he here, alone, with you?"

"He's Eli. He's Elizabeth Daleiden's eighteen-year-old son. He came here to let me know how angry he was."

"Angry? He didn't look angry."

"I don't blame him. I'd be angry, too. I'm a blundering, interfering asshole."

Frank laughed again. "At least you admit it. What did you do this time?"

"My visit to see his mother is going to lead to her indictment for murder—for three murders, actually."

Frank became uncharacteristically serious.

"God, Jonah, that *was* a blunder."

*****

Jonah called Elizabeth's attorney, took a day off work and drove out to Oxford to see her in her office.

Violet Sutherland graduated from the University of Illinois Law School five years before Jonah and Frank did. She began her conversation with Jonah by telling him he'd no doubt be a witness for the prosecution.

"Please don't construe anything I say as a request for you to alter your testimony," she said. "All I, as Elizabeth Daleiden's attorney, can expect is that you'll tell the truth."

"That's all I intend to do," Jonah said. "I've never handled a criminal case, but I can't imagine how my testimony will help convict Elizabeth of murders she never committed. She only told me she was certain Henry and Titus weren't killed by a mob."

"Or by an intruder."

"Or by an intruder. I believe she still can't face having failed to protect her friends. So she denies any murder took place. And the fire has to be just what the cowardly authorities at the time said it was: a dreadful accident."

Violet told Jonah she grew up with two brothers on a farm west of Oxford. Their landlord was a doctor in Chicago who personally collected the rent each month. Violet had to pay for college and law school without any help from her family. In college she worked in a dormitory cafeteria. In law school she was a dorm counselor and part-time teaching assistant.

When Violet graduated from law school in 1969, she moved into the apartment above the bookstore on Main Street in Oxford. She'd lived there ever since with Belle Remington, her friend in high school and roommate in college. Belle was the daughter of the president of the Oxford National Bank. She'd received the store as a gift from her mother and father when she graduated from the University of Illinois at Champaign-Urbana with a bachelor's degree in English literature in 1966. Violet earned a bachelor's degree the same day. Hers was in history.

At thirty-three, Violet was, like Jonah and Frank, a physically active lawyer. She told Jonah she and Belle stocked the bookstore shelves together, kept a large vegetable garden behind the store, and rode their bicycles into the countryside and back every day the weather allowed.

"So that's your theory of the case, Jonah?" Violet asked. "Elizabeth can't admit an intruder or two, or a mob, killed Henry and Titus because then she'd also have to admit she failed to protect those two old gay men who were her friends—such close friends they even left her their farm?"

"That's the only reason I can see for her to deny what obviously happened."

Violet's face was so expressionless Jonah couldn't tell whether she found his remark insightful or ridiculous.

"Do you expect to attend the trial, Jonah? I mean, the whole trial, not just the part when you testify?"

"Yes, I do. I'm certain Elizabeth is innocent. I can't believe a jury could be so cruel as to convict her of murder—and subject her to the possibility of spending the rest of her life in prison. And losing her farm. I simply can't believe it."

"I'm glad to hear you'll be with us. But I feel I should warn you about a question I'm going to ask you on cross-examination."

Jonah sat motionless in his chair. Reporters from the Chicago television stations and newspapers would be present in the courtroom. Because the Illinois Supreme Court didn't allow cameras and microphones inside a courtroom, the media people would be waiting to accost the witnesses on the long flight of steps outside the courthouse.

Jonah had to admit, to himself at least, he'd grown fearful.

"I'm going to ask you," Violet continued, "if you're gay."

"And I'm going to tell you," Jonah said, "I'm damned glad I'm gay."

"I'm also going to ask you if you're out to prove a Concord County mob burned down the house of two old gay men with them in it twenty-two years ago."

"And I'm going to tell you that's precisely what I'm out to do. I was six years old. I was there with my grandmother. I heard what those people were saying. I saw the mob with my own eyes. I don't need more proof."

*****

"Unfortunately," Violet said, "what Eli told you is true. Tanner Howland assures me his people have found other evidence that will prove to a jury Elizabeth murdered Henry and Titus as well as her father."

Tanner Howland was the Concord County state's attorney.

"He tells me," Violet said, "he's glad he can't ask for the death penalty for her. But he also says he'll demand she gets life in prison unless she does the right thing and pleads guilty."

"That's crazy. She'll never plead guilty."

"No, she won't. And I'd never advise her to do that."

"But what on earth," Jonah asked, "is Tanner's other evidence?"

"He won't tell me. I assume you know he isn't required to. In the criminal court we don't have the discovery you civil lawyers take for granted. We'll have to wait until the trial to find out what Tanner's evidence is. In the meantime, Elizabeth and I can only guess what he has. We've come up with some ideas. But she and I will have to prepare for each and every possibility. We won't dare leave anything out. We'll be spending a lot of time together in the next few months."

Jonah knew what he had to do.

"I agree with you one hundred percent on the main thing, Jonah. Elizabeth is innocent."

*****

Jonah took a detour to Revere on his way home from Oxford. Eli was finishing his chores, which at that time of the day consisted of feeding four hundred hogs the ground corn and oats they loved. Elizabeth was in the house fixing supper.

Jonah picked up a couple of five-gallon pails, filled them and began helping Eli.

"I assume you and your mother share the farmwork."

"Yeah, we do."

"I understand she's going to be busy with her lawyer for the next few months, the same months you've got a lot of field work to do here. And you told me you're planning to start college at Northern in September. Have you thought how you're going to handle all that?"

"I've thought about it a lot. I'm going to work my ass off. My mother is innocent. I have to do everything I can to keep her from being convicted of murder and sent to prison for the rest of her life."

"Yeah, you do."

"I might have to put off college."

"I don't think you should do that."

"I might have no choice."

"What if I give you a choice?"

*****

Eli and Jonah were putting their pails away when Elizabeth appeared at the door to the barn. She knew Jonah had come out to see her lawyer that afternoon. She'd also recognized his car in the driveway.

"Can you join us for supper, Jonah?" she asked.

"Don't even try to say no," Eli said.

"Then I'll say yes," Jonah said.

Chapter Five

Elizabeth and Eli set a place for Jonah at their kitchen table. They kept chickens and a vegetable garden for themselves. Supper that evening was a roast chicken and a salad with the first leaf lettuce, radishes, asparagus and green onions of the spring. They'd lightly roasted the radishes, asparagus and onions with the chicken.

"That bird," Eli told Jonah, "is one less rooster crowing at sunrise. He was still young, though. He should be tender."

Elizabeth looked at Jonah and laughed. "We keep the chickens in Henry and Titus's old coop. We can scarcely hear them this far away."

"My grandmother and I kept chickens," Jonah said. "We had a garden, too."

"I remember your grandmother sold eggs," Elizabeth said. "I'd see her delivering them in Revere. Weren't you still selling them after she became ill?"

"Yeah, but most of our egg customers had taken pity on us by then. They came out to the farm to pick them up."

Eli had a rhubarb pie baking in the oven. He told Jonah he'd put it together the previous evening, using the first pickings of the season for the dessert as well as the salad.

Elizabeth looked at Jonah again. "Eli says you want to help us. Can I ask you what you have in mind?"

"I want to help you with your farmwork. I think it's the best thing I can do right now—the best way I can help keep an innocent person out of prison."

"You want to be our hired man?" Eli asked.

"An unpaid hired man," Jonah said. "You've got a lot to do here. I see you're about to start planting at least a hundred and fifty acres of corn. You don't have the most recent equipment to do it, either."

"Our farm is rather labor-intensive," Elizabeth said. "That's mostly by choice. Before Daniel found out he had a kind of cancer nobody could cure, we had three able bodies to do our farmwork. We didn't need to spend money on the latest machinery. To tell you the truth, I don't care for some of the things I see farmers do nowadays."

"Like locking their livestock up in tiny pens," Eli said, "and never letting them see the light of day."

"I've heard about that," Jonah said, looking at Eli. "Anyway, you can't plant all that corn by yourself. You've got to finish high school. Your mother has to spend her days with Violet. And I'm the person responsible for that. You told me so yourself. I think I'd better help you every day you need me. We raised hogs on my grandmother's farm. You can't say I won't know what to do on yours. Where do you sell your hay?"

"To an Italian guy from Chicago," Eli said. "He comes out and picks it up in his truck and takes it to the racetracks."

"Tony Marino," Elizabeth said.

"Good," Jonah said. "He still pays the highest prices?"

"As long as you plant what he wants you to," Eli said.

"Lots of timothy for the horses," Jonah said. "That explains what I saw in your hayfield. I'd like to help you bale it."

"We can't let you do that kind of work, Jonah," Elizabeth said. "Baling hay? Good lord, you're a lawyer in a big firm in Chicago. You can't come out here and spend your valuable time working without pay."

"I'm no longer a lawyer in a big firm in Chicago," Jonah said. "I gave them my notice. I'm taking the rest of the week to clear my desk. I can help you start planting your corn on Saturday."

Elizabeth and Eli both stared at Jonah.

"Why in hell did you quit your job?" Eli asked.

"They would've fired me anyway," Jonah replied.

He turned to Elizabeth.

"Your lawyer is going to do something I wholeheartedly believe she should do. When she cross-examines me in your trial, she's going to ask if I'm gay."

"Oh, no," Elizabeth said.

"Oh, yes," Jonah countered. "And she should, if it'll help your case. I don't know for sure what Violet is thinking, and she didn't tell me. She's your lawyer, not mine. I assume, though, she'll try to make the jury think I'm a wild-eyed gay man who's out to prove something horrible happened twenty-two years ago. A mob killed two gay men who'd been passing themselves off as brothers, and then they set their house on fire for good measure. I also expect she'll attempt to portray you as the men's friend who knew they were gay, but you still can't believe a mob in Concord County would ever do what I'm convinced that one did. In any event, if your attorney thinks it'll help your case to expose me to the jury, and to the world, as a gay man, deluded or not, demanding justice be done, then I want her to do it."

Elizabeth shook her head.

"What's your testimony got to do with your job?" Eli asked.

"Everything," Jonah replied. "Violet agrees with me on what will happen when the grand jury gives Tanner Howland what he wants—which is three indictments for murder. The media will see a pleasant, private, recently widowed woman working her farm with her teenage son suddenly revealed to be a cold-blooded killer. Who might very well be taken from her quiet Concord County farm—and the son she so dearly loves—and sent to prison for the rest of her life. What a story that will be. If your mother did what Tanner claims she did, nobody's mother, no matter how saintly, would be above suspicion."

Elizabeth turned to Eli. "Violet told me that, too. The Chicago television stations and newspapers will ask us for as much information as we'll give them. I'm following her instructions to the letter. She doesn't want me to be seen as uncooperative with the media. That would make me look guilty. On the other hand, she doesn't want me to say anything we'll regret."

Jonah also turned to Eli. "The reporters will be in court the day I testify. I plan to say I'm happy I'm gay. I also intend to testify that when I came to see your mother, I'd decided as a gay man I couldn't remain silent any longer. Not about what I believed I'd witnessed twenty-two years ago: two men murdered by their neighbors for nothing more than loving one another."

Jonah could smell the rhubarb pie baking in the oven.

"The people in that law firm I work for," he said, "would realize what a big mistake they made when they hired me. I'd hardly be the first lawyer they got rid of for being gay. I've heard how they do it. They wouldn't come right out and fire me. They'd take me off the team doing the bank's work. They'd throw me in with the lawyers examining endless file drawers of possible evidence in some extremely boring antitrust litigation. They've always got at least one of those cases going. That's what they do with new lawyers and lawyers out of favor, lawyers who'll never make partner. But maybe in my case they'd just fire me and be done with it. They could always say they didn't need the kind of publicity I was bringing down on them."

Jonah used his knife and fork to cut a slender stalk of asparagus.

"Your roast chicken is wonderful," he said. "So is your salad. I wanted to quit that job anyway. Everything I did for that firm was boring, even if it wasn't antitrust litigation. I'm sure I can find something more interesting and worthwhile to do."

*****

"What kind of job will you be looking for now, Jonah?" Elizabeth asked.

"I won't be looking for a job," Jonah replied. "Not until after your trial is over and a jury has acquitted you."

Elizabeth sighed. "We don't know when that will be. Will you be all right? Please let me know if I'm raising questions you'd rather not discuss with Eli and me. But I do mean financially."

"After the trouble I've brought down on you," Jonah said, "I'll speak with you about anything you wish. I assume you know I sold the farm after my grandmother died and I finished high school. I closed on it within a week after I graduated."

"Yes," Elizabeth said. "Daniel and I heard about that. We were sorry to learn you were leaving Revere. You took such good care of your grandmother in her final years and did all the work on her farm."

Eli looked at Jonah. "You owned a farm when you were eighteen?"

"He inherited his grandmother's farm when she died," Elizabeth said. "How old were you then, Jonah?"

"I was seventeen. I finished picking the corn that year the day she died. The court had to appoint the Revere State Bank to act as my guardian."

"Yes," Elizabeth said. "Daniel and I heard about that, too. You spent most of your last year in high school living by yourself on your grandmother's farm."

"When I sold the farm," Jonah said, "I had to pay the bills from the attorneys, the doctors, the hospital and the funeral home. They all had liens on the property. And it was only an eighty-acre farm. Still, I left Revere with what I hoped was enough money to get me through college and law school."

"Was it?" Eli asked.

Jonah smiled. "I only spent part of it on college and law school. I worked at part-time jobs all during those years. When I started with the big firm in Chicago, I used what was left of my grandmother's money to buy the two-flat where I've lived ever since. My tenant, my friend, pays me more than enough in rent to cover the taxes and insurance. So I've been able to save some money. I can get by without a job for a while."

"Thank you for that explanation," Elizabeth said. "It makes me feel better about accepting your offer."

"The only thing I want to do now is help you and Eli," Jonah said. "And by help, I do mean planting your corn, baling your hay and feeding your hogs."

Elizabeth turned to Eli.

"I'm sure you remember Daniel and me talking about the boy who fired his grandmother's hired man. We heard Jonah had good cause to do it, too. The hired man was playing poker in the back room of a tavern in Oxford when he should've been feeding hogs on a farm in Revere. Jonah tells me he was only thirteen when he did that."

"Yeah," Eli said, "I remember you and Dad talking about that boy."

*****

Eli removed his rhubarb pie from the oven and placed it in front of his mother for her to slice. He took a bowl of vanilla ice cream out of the freezer and put it on the table. He'd also made that the night before. He and his mother kept a cow as well as chickens and a garden.

"I hope you'll forgive something I did," Jonah said to Elizabeth. "But when I was in Oxford today I went to the county recorder's office. I saw the mortgage papers you and Daniel signed before he died—as well as those you signed after he died. I could see what his illness did to you and Eli financially. Please forgive me if you didn't want that known."

"There's nothing to forgive," Elizabeth said. "Those are

documents the public has a right to see. Why should I object to your seeing them?"

"My parents took me with them when they signed those papers," Eli said. "I knew what they were doing. They told me they were borrowing against what they'd hoped would someday be mine. I told them, if they left me nothing at all, they'd have no need to justify themselves. I still believe that."

Jonah turned to Elizabeth.

"And now you'll have substantial attorney fees to pay."

"Violet said she wished she could represent me for free," Elizabeth said. "But she can't. She's had to turn away any new clients and any new business from her current clients. I insisted on her charging me what she'd charge anybody else. When she isn't meeting with me, she's out interviewing potential witnesses. She's talking with all the older neighbors in Revere Township—all those who remember the night of the fire and the day of my father's death."

"I can imagine what she's doing," Jonah said. "I believe she's well worth the money you'll pay her. But it's another good reason for me to help you with your work."

Eli passed the ice cream to his mother.

"I think we should give Jonah a chance," he said. "I'd like to see what he can do. He's in great shape. He might prove himself to be pretty useful. But even if he won't let us pay him for his work, he should at least take his meals with us when he's here."

Elizabeth smiled. "I'm afraid we can't force Jonah to eat with us. But I hope he does. I second your invitation. It's the least we can do."

"After your meal this evening," Jonah said, "I'd find it difficult to turn you down. I'll say yes to that. You'll have to let me help wash and dry the dishes, though. I can prepare a noisy rooster for the oven, too. I can also help you weed your garden, feed your chickens, gather your eggs and milk your cow."

Elizabeth and Eli laughed.

"We'll be glad to let you do all those things," Eli said.

Chapter **Six**

The next weekend Eli, Elizabeth and Jonah began planting corn. Jonah drove out to Revere in the mornings and back to Chicago in the evenings after supper.

On Monday morning Jonah testified before the grand jury in Oxford. The hearing was closed to the public. Not even Elizabeth or her attorney could attend. Concord County State's Attorney Tanner Howland asked all the questions.

Afterward, Jonah walked the short distance from the courthouse to Violet's office.

"Tanner seemed pleased with my testimony," he reported.

"I'm sure he was," Violet said. "He only wanted you to tell the grand jury what Elizabeth told you."

"He appeared to be surprised, though, when I testified I'd given up my job in Chicago. He asked me if I'm looking for another position. I simply told him I am. He didn't ask how actively I'm looking."

Violet smiled. "I wonder what he'll think when he learns his witness is helping the accused and her son with the work on their farm."

*****

On Thursday morning the grand jury handed down three indictments, one for each of the victims Elizabeth Daleiden supposedly murdered.

That afternoon Jonah went with Elizabeth and Eli to the courthouse in Oxford to attend a bail bond proceeding Tanner and Violet had agreed to.

Eli wore the dark blue suit Jonah and Elizabeth had picked out for him in the men's clothing store in Oxford. Eli hadn't previously felt a need to own a suit. Elizabeth said he'd want one anyway for his high school graduation ceremony.

Elizabeth wore a plain, light-blue cotton dress with comfortable low-heeled shoes. And not even a visit to a court to face murder charges could induce her to apply makeup or bother with jewelry.

"Do you think," Eli asked Jonah, "it's one of those less-is-more things?"

Jonah laughed. "It could be."

Tanner was aware no judge would find Elizabeth a flight risk and deny her bail altogether. Such an order would force Elizabeth to spend the entire time before and during her trial in the Concord County jail. Tanner had therefore agreed to accept a lien on her farm as bail. If Elizabeth fled and didn't show up for her trial, the county would sell her farm, pay off the prior liens for Daniel's medical expenses and keep the rest of the money for itself.

Violet had prepared the papers. Elizabeth and Tanner would sign them as soon as the judge agreed.

When Jonah walked into the courtroom with Elizabeth and Eli, Tanner, sitting at the counsel table for the prosecuting attorneys, gave him a long, wondering look.

Violet, sitting at the counsel table for the defendant, glanced at Tanner and smiled.

Tanner presented no witnesses in support of the bail bond order he'd agreed to.

Eli was Violet's only witness. He testified Northern Illinois University had accepted his application for admission. He intended to continue living with his mother on her farm and drive back and forth to his classes in DeKalb.

"Eli," Judge Gideon Heidecker asked, "do you also intend to continue helping your mother with the work on her farm?"

"Yes, sir, I do."

The chief judge of the circuit court that included Concord County had selected Gideon, a life-long resident of Oxford Township—like Violet and Tanner—to hear Elizabeth's case.

Gideon, Violet had informed Jonah, was the same age as Elizabeth, forty-five. He appeared to Jonah to be one judge who lifted weights and ran. With his six-foot-two height, square jaw, dark wavy hair and blue eyes, he was the kind of older man even Frank would have sex with, show off to Jonah the next morning and mention afterward every chance he got.

"Your mother's farm is how large?" Gideon asked Eli.

"Three hundred twenty acres."

"You and your mother have done all the work on a three-hundred-twenty-acre farm since—"

"Since my father's cancer got so bad he couldn't work anymore," Eli said. "He died last Christmas. I'm sorry, Judge, for

36

interrupting you."

"That's all right," Gideon said. "I was sorry to hear your father died."

He glanced at Elizabeth before he returned his attention to Eli.

"I grew up on a farm," he said, "but we were tenants. Why don't you and your mother rent yours out and let somebody else do the work?"

"My mother doesn't wish to be a landlady," Eli replied. "She's a farmer. So am I."

Gideon looked at Violet.

"I'll sign your order," he said.

He did so, handed it to his clerk and turned to Eli.

"You and your mother can go home now."

He and Eli were both in tears.

*****

Violet said somebody in Tanner's office, obviously doing what the boss wanted done, had tipped off the media.

Reporters from the Chicago television stations and newspapers were in the courtroom for the bail bond hearing. They were waiting with their camera people on the front steps when Elizabeth, Violet, Eli, Jonah and Violet's partner Belle came out of the courthouse.

One of the reporters knew who Jonah was, but she didn't know why he was with the defendant and her son.

Elizabeth read a statement: "I didn't murder my father. Nor did I murder my neighbors, Henry and Titus. I expect the truth to come out at my trial. I anticipate testifying myself. My lawyer, Violet Sutherland, has advised me I shouldn't say anything more at this time. I'm sorry I can't speak with you further."

"Eli, what can you tell us?" the television reporter who knew Jonah asked. "Is your mother innocent or guilty?"

The reporter, Jill Foster, had been in the same class in law school with Jonah and Frank.

"My mother is innocent," Eli said. "My mother's attorney hasn't told me what I can or can't say to you. She isn't my attorney. But that's all I'll say to you now—my mother is innocent."

"You reduced the judge to tears," Jill said, glancing at Jonah.

"Please let us pass," Eli said. "We've got to go home now. We have a lot of work to do on our farm."

The reporters and camera people parted to make a path for Elizabeth and her entourage to walk down the courthouse steps.

Eli shook hands with and said "thank you" to each of the reporters he passed.

Tanner, waiting patiently at the top of the stairs, was up next for the media.

*****

After Jonah returned home that night, he watched a late television newscast with Frank.

They saw Elizabeth, Eli and Violet on the courthouse steps. They heard Jill's questions and Elizabeth's and Eli's responses.

Despite his attempt to stay out of view, Jonah was briefly visible in one shot.

After the newscast went to a commercial, Frank turned to Jonah.

"I must say your friends handled that quite well," Frank said. "Everybody will wonder why this innocent-seeming mother of such an innocent and loyal son has been charged with murdering three people who were so close to her."

"Well, she is innocent," Jonah said. "Even a hard-boiled cynic like you can see that."

"You still don't know what she's hiding?"

"I have no doubt Elizabeth hasn't told me the whole story. I haven't spoken a word to her about her father's death. On the other hand, I'll believe the story she tells when she tells it. Now, as you know, the only person she should tell the whole truth to is her attorney. And I'm not her attorney, only her unpaid hired man."

Frank laughed. "Her son's boyfriend posing as her unpaid hired man. Did Eli know that by himself, that business about his mother's attorney not being his attorney?"

"I've told you," Jonah said, "Eli is an intelligent young man. I don't recall giving him the legalistic insight he shared with the media, but Violet might've."

"He tells the reporters he doesn't have an attorney, but I'm damned sure at least two attorneys advised him to say as little as possible—and it never hurts to be nice to the reporters."

Frank looked at Jonah and snickered.

"This Eli is the real reason you've involved yourself so deeply in their world."

Jonah shook his head. "Eli isn't my boyfriend. He's never given me any reason to think he's gay. Therefore, I can only assume he's straight. So no matter what other outstanding qualities he possesses, I can't waste my time dreaming about him and me becoming boyfriends."

"Oh, bullshit. He's perfect for you. He's young, cute and innocent. He might be straight, but he still hasn't come right out and told you that. And he's a farm boy. Let's face it. You're in love with him."

"I've never imagined having sex with Eli, let alone falling in love with him."

Frank laughed. "Liar, liar, your pants are on fire. And here's another house with two gay men in it that's going up in flames. You told me you were giving up the chase. You wanted a boyfriend."

"That's still true," Jonah said.

"And this Eli is the one you've come up with. You've always been my hero. I hope you know that."

"Eli isn't my boyfriend. How many times do I have to say it?"

"As many times as you wish, Jonah. I'd never try to stop you. But saying it won't make it so."

Jonah had to wash that down with some wine.

"Isn't this Eli," Frank asked, "the son of the farmer you liked so much growing up? You told me you adored the man."

"I told you that."

Frank looked at Jonah with a grin on his face.

"And this Eli," Frank said, "is that man's lovely son."

"His name is Eli—not 'this Eli.'"

*****

"Gideon went to DePaul," Violet said. "For both college and law school. His family was Catholic. They were poor, too. He must've gotten scholarships."

Elizabeth and Eli had invited Violet and Belle to share wine and supper with them and Jonah on Saturday evening.

Eli and Jonah had spent another long day in the fields.

Elizabeth and Violet spent as much time that day in Violet's office.

Tanner had released a list of the witnesses who'd testified before the grand jury. Neither Elizabeth nor Violet recognized the names of two of them.

Was it possible, Violet wondered, those two witnesses—along with a third witness, Olivia Daleiden—would provide the additional evidence Tanner needed to convict Elizabeth? If so, what was the evidence? Violet and Elizabeth had to figure that out.

"Gideon's wife," Violet continued, "was his classmate at Oxford High School."

"She went to Northwestern for college," Belle said. "Her family could afford it. They were Episcopalian. Then she came home to Oxford and taught school. Violet and I had her for our teacher in seventh grade. We loved her. She encouraged our most outlandish dreams. I told her I wanted to read every good book ever written. Violet confided she wanted to be a lawyer. And this was in the Fifties. Gideon's wife was ahead of her time. She told us women could do everything men could do."

"When did she marry Gideon?" Elizabeth asked.

"It had to have been 1957," Belle replied. "It was the summer after we had her in seventh grade. And the summer after he graduated from law school. Twenty years ago."

"They had just the one child, the boy?" Elizabeth asked.

"Just the one," Belle said.

Violet turned to Eli and Jonah. "I'm sorry. You don't know what we're talking about."

"Oh, but I believe I do," Jonah said. "I thought I'd heard his name before. That dreadful business? The victims were his wife and child?"

"What happened?" Eli asked.

Belle squeezed his hand.

"Gideon's wife," she said, "was walking across a street in downtown Oxford with their son in her arms. A man who'd been drinking too much ran a red light and hit them. Violet and I went to their

40

funeral."

"The guy was speeding, too," Violet said. "Witnesses saw him do it. He killed them instantly. But a judge only found him guilty of traffic offenses and fined him. He had political connections. He never spent a day in jail. Unlike the drunk, Gideon had no connections. But he was the youngest judge ever elected in Concord County. Nobody dared run against him."

"I remember when that was in the news," Elizabeth said. "I noticed their boy was the same age as Eli. He'd be graduating from high school now. Has Gideon remarried?"

Belle shook her head. "People who know him say he never will."

Jonah wondered who'd first reduced the other to tears that day. The witness who was the same age the judge's son would've been? Or the judge who'd reminded the witness of his deceased father?

Chapter Seven

"FARMER'S WIDOW INDICTED FOR THREE MURDERS," one headline read the morning after the grand jury handed down its indictments and Judge Heidecker let Elizabeth Daleiden, the "farmer's widow," remain free on bail. "Cases 22 and 27 Years Old" was one sub-headline. "State's Attorney Says She Killed Her Own Father" was another.

*****

Jill Foster found the name of her law school classmate, Jonah Neumeyer, on Tanner's list of grand jury witnesses. That explained his presence at Elizabeth Daleiden's bail bond hearing. But if he was a witness for the prosecution, why was he with Elizabeth and her son and attorney?

Jill finally reached Jonah on his telephone Sunday evening when he arrived home from Revere. Could she interview him?

After calling Violet and Elizabeth, Jonah agreed to an interview with Jill. He suggested they do it in his backyard garden early the next morning, which was supposed to be warm and sunny. Jill thought that was an excellent proposal.

Jill and Jonah sat in two of his lawn chairs. The cameraman did most of his shooting sitting in another lawn chair in front of them. His shots often included Jonah's and Frank's azaleas and irises in bloom behind them.

Jill spoke first, looking directly at the camera.

"Imagine my surprise," she said, "when I read the list of grand jury witnesses in the case of the Concord County farmer's widow indicted for committing three murders. I found the name of a classmate of mine in law school. I'm with Jonah Neumeyer now in his beautiful garden in Lincoln Park, and he's ready to speak with us about the case of Elizabeth Daleiden, the farmer's widow."

Jill and the camera turned to Jonah.

"I understand, Jonah," Jill said, "when you graduated from law school, you went to work for one of the largest law firms in Chicago. Do you still work for that firm, Jonah?"

"No," Jonah replied. "I recently resigned my position."

Jill couldn't conceal her surprise.

"Why did you do that?" she asked.

"I did it so I could help Elizabeth Daleiden and her son, Eli, with the work on their farm. I grew up on a farm near theirs. So I'm familiar with what they do."

"Why do they need your help?"

"Elizabeth is busy with her attorney preparing for her trial. Her son Eli will soon graduate from high school, but in September he'll go to college. They badly need my help. And I'm more than ready to give it to them."

"Isn't it rather odd, Jonah, that the prosecutor will likely call you as his witness in a triple-murder case and yet you've given up your job in a big Chicago law firm to help the defendant and her son with their farmwork?"

Jonah turned to face the camera.

"Elizabeth Daleiden has never murdered anybody," he said. "The Concord County state's attorney, Tanner Howland, sought the murder indictments solely for political reasons. He's running for an open congressional seat next year, and I understand he'll have a strong opponent in the Republican primary. If he obtains murder convictions against Elizabeth Daleiden, they'll be totally unjust, unspeakable, unthinkable. But they'll give Tanner Howland the publicity he needs to go to Washington. And that's what this case is all about: publicity for Tanner Howland."

Jonah could see, out of the corner of his eye, Jill was delighted with what she'd found in his garden on a lovely Monday morning in May.

"But Jonah," she said, "you testified for State's Attorney Tanner Howland before the grand jury. You're on his list of witnesses."

"I told the grand jury the truth, Jill. I didn't testify for or against anybody."

"Do you know if Tanner Howland intends to call you to testify at Elizabeth Daleiden's trial?"

"I'm quite certain he will. But again, I'll only tell the truth. I won't testify for or against anybody."

"Can you tell us what you told the grand jury and what you'll tell the trial jury?"

"I could tell you, Jill, but I don't think I should. If you attend

Elizabeth Daleiden's trial—and I hope you do—you'll hear what I have to say. Now if you don't mind, I really should be going. This is a school day for Eli, and Elizabeth is with her lawyer. They're working long hours on her defense, as they should. I've got a lot to do when I get out to Revere this morning."

*****

After Jill's exclusive interview with Jonah played, Tanner angrily denied pursuing murder charges against Elizabeth for political reasons.

"I'd never disgrace the office of the Concord County state's attorney by doing such a thing," he thundered in his best baritone voice. "Mr. Neumeyer might be understandably upset that his own testimony helped lead to three murder indictments against a person he considers a friend, but that's no excuse for him to slander me. Politics plays absolutely no part in what I do as the state's attorney of Concord County."

The other television and newspaper reporters following the case called Jonah at his home and at Elizabeth and Eli's house demanding interviews with him. He agreed to one interview with all of them but only if they left him and Elizabeth and Eli strictly alone afterward to do their work and prepare for the trial. He chose to see them at Elizabeth's farm on an afternoon Eli was still in school and Elizabeth was with Violet.

He showed up for the interview on the lawn in front of the house wearing his work clothes—a white tee shirt, Levi's and gym shoes.

He freely repeated his "slander" of Tanner.

"Aren't you afraid he'll sue you?" one reporter asked.

"No," Jonah replied. "In a slander suit, the truth is always a defense. Tanner knows that."

Jonah knew even better that Tanner wouldn't wish to focus the attention of potential jurors and voters on the political aspects of Elizabeth Daleiden's triple-murder case.

Jonah repeated all his other answers to Jill's questions and declined once again to discuss his past or future testimony. He thanked all the people present, including the sheriff's deputies, for not stepping on Elizabeth and Eli's flower beds and excused himself to get back to work.

Most of the reporters went straight to Oxford to ask Tanner for a response. In particular, they wanted Tanner's reaction to Jonah's remark that in a slander suit the truth was always a defense. Tanner agreed to another press conference on the courthouse steps.

"I won't engage in a tit for tat with Mr. Neumeyer," Tanner said. "I do intend to call him as a witness in Elizabeth Daleiden's trial. And all I expect from him is that he'll tell the trial jury what he told the grand jury. If he doesn't, I'll seek his indictment for perjury."

*****

Elizabeth spent the day after Eli's graduation from high school with Violet.

Jonah and Eli ate lunch together in the Daleiden kitchen. They had all the windows wide open, the better to catch the breeze.

"I have a question for you," Eli said.

"Who are you reporting for?" Jonah asked, laughing.

"This isn't a laughing matter," Eli said.

"Sorry," Jonah said. "Ask me your question."

"Why do you always talk about your grandmother as if you had no other relatives?"

Jonah took a deep breath.

"My parents died when I was one year old. My grandfather died when I was two. Needless to say, I don't remember them. I had no brothers or sisters. My mother was an only child. I have grandparents, aunts, uncles and cousins on my father's side, but I've never met any of them."

Eli and Jonah were eating the leftover meat of another unlucky rooster, together with asparagus and onions from the garden in a sauce they'd concocted using leftover cheese.

"People tell some wild stories about your mother and father," Eli said.

"I'm sure they do."

"So what's the true story?"

"My parents fucked when they were sixteen. They were living

46

on neighboring farms just down the road from here. My father didn't bother to wear a condom. And my mother didn't have a pill to take back then. He was one of four children of tenant farmers. She was the daughter of the owners of an eighty-acre hog farm. She got pregnant. The high school principal expelled them both the day he found out."

Eli shook his head.

Jonah continued his story.

"My father promised my mother he'd marry her as soon as he legally could, with his parents' consent, which was when he turned eighteen. He came to see her and their one-year-old son, me, on his eighteenth birthday. That's when he told her he wouldn't marry her. He'd fallen in love with—and hoped to marry—somebody else."

"God," Eli said.

"My mother found her father's double-barreled shotgun in the basement. She confronted my father. He was sitting in an easy chair in the living room speaking with her parents, my grandparents. She pulled one trigger and killed him. When the deputy sheriffs showed up to arrest her, she pulled the other trigger and killed herself."

"That's what people say. Your mother killed your father when he refused to marry her and make you legitimate. That's how it happened?"

Eli and Jonah had both paused eating their chicken and asparagus.

"That's what my grandmother told me," Jonah said. "She was there. She saw and heard everything. She had no reason to lie to me. I was there, too, sitting on my grandmother's lap. But I don't remember anything, of course."

"What happened to your relatives on your father's side?"

"They left Revere. Their landlord refused to renew their lease. They never acknowledged me as a grandchild or nephew anyway. They claimed my father had told them my mother was a whore. Anybody could've been my father, they said. I've never been able to find out where they went. They apparently didn't want anybody to know."

Eli shook his head. "That's a damned sad story. My mother told me she and my father and your parents were classmates in grade school and high school in Revere."

"Yeah, they were—up to the day my parents got their asses

kicked out."

"Who was the other person your father fell in love with?"

Jonah shook his head. "We don't need to talk about that."

"Do you know who the person was?"

"My grandmother told me. She also told me nobody else needed to know—and especially not the other young woman."

"Can I guess?"

"I'd rather we didn't say anything more about it."

"The other woman your father fell in love with—and hoped to marry instead of your mother—was my mother?"

Jonah sighed. "My father told my grandparents his newly beloved, Elizabeth Reifert, would soon realize she couldn't marry a Catholic like Daniel Daleiden. His mother—your grandmother Olivia— would never allow it. My father said he intended to give Elizabeth plenty of reasons to forget Daniel existed. That's when my mother shot him."

"God, Jonah."

*****

The day after Eli's graduation from high school was also the day he began to insist Jonah stay overnight at his mother's house, at least during their busiest times. He said Jonah was "senselessly" driving back and forth between Chicago and Revere every day.

"You don't need to do that," Eli said at the supper table that evening.

"I think Eli's right," Elizabeth said. "You're wasting gasoline and your time on all that driving."

Jonah looked at Elizabeth and knew he had to terminate the conversation or deeply regret his failure to do so.

"I appreciate your offer," he said, "but you only have two beds in your house. And I'm not much good at sleeping on a couch or the floor. And I won't ask either of you to give up your bed."

Elizabeth scoffed. "You can sleep with Eli. His bed is large enough for both of you."

Jonah turned to Eli.

"I don't care how big his bed is. I don't want to be a twenty-eight-year-old gay man in the same bed with an eighteen-year-old straight guy."

Elizabeth laughed. "I don't think you'll need to worry about that."

Eli looked at Jonah and laughed himself.

Was he, Jonah wondered, smirking?

Toward the end of the meal, Eli brought up the subject again.

"Are you going to do the sensible thing, Jonah, and stay overnight here?"

"I'll bring some things with me tomorrow. I'll give it a try. But believe me, I'm not doing it to get in bed with you."

Elizabeth and Eli looked at one another and laughed again.

Chapter Eight

Eli and Jonah both decided to shave and shower before they went to bed. They agreed it would save them time in the morning.

Jonah used the bathroom adjoining Eli's bedroom. Eli used the first-floor bathroom.

With towels pulled tight around their waists, they met in Eli's bedroom for what Jonah knew would be a confrontation.

"Okay," Jonah said, "which side of the bed is your favorite? The window side or the door side?"

Eli laughed. "If I had to choose, I'd say the window side."

"Great. That will be your side. That third of the bed nearest the window. This is my side, the third of it nearest the door."

Eli stared at the bed. "What about the middle third?"

"That remains empty, untouched—a no-man's-land."

Eli laughed again. "What's your problem, Jonah? I can stay on my side of the bed without having it mapped out for me. Are you worried about yourself?"

"Of course not."

"Then what are you worried about?"

"Being misled."

"You? Jonah Neumeyer? The love child who fired his grand-mother's hired man when he was thirteen? I think not."

Eli removed his towel, draped it over the towel rack in his bath-room and walked naked to his side of the bed.

He got what he wanted.

Jonah couldn't take his eyes off him.

Making no attempt to hide his smirk this time, Eli eased himself between the sheets on his third of the bed.

"Don't you sleep naked, Jonah?"

"I do. Tonight, though, I thought I'd put on some clean under-wear."

Once again, Eli laughed.

"Because you're in a bed with me? Really, Jonah, you're going too far. Take your towel off, hang it on the rack in the bathroom where I hung mine and get into this bed naked. I want you to feel like you're at home here. I'm ready for a good night's sleep. We've got a lot to do tomorrow. I never thought just getting in bed with me would frighten you so much."

Jonah found himself obeying his host, who openly stared at him after he was naked.

The nightstand light was on Jonah's side of the bed. Lying on his right side with his back to Eli, he turned off the lamp with his left hand.

As soon as the room went dark, Eli slid across the no-man's-land and ran his hands up and down Jonah's back.

Jonah, as if paralyzed by snake venom, remained motionless.

Eli pressed his body against Jonah's.

Jonah still refused to respond.

Eli reached around Jonah with his left hand and caressed his pectoral muscles and tits. Then he let his hand go lower down, past Jonah's abdominal muscles, to touch the part of his body no straight man—not even one out to tease an easily misled gay man—would consider touching, especially in its present condition.

Jonah turned himself over, met Eli face-to-face and gave him the exuberant kiss he'd wanted to give him the moment he walked into his house in April.

Eli gasped.

Jonah pulled back a bit.

"Is this what you want?" he asked.

"Yeah," Eli said. "With you, Jonah. I have to warn you, though, I've never done anything like this before."

"I understand," Jonah said. "We won't do anything you're not ready to do."

"We've got to get off, though," Eli insisted. "Both of us."

"Yeah," Jonah said, "we'll do that. I can guarantee it."

*****

After they did, Eli continued trespassing in the no-man's-land, lying with his body pressed against Jonah's the rest of the night.

While they were feeding the hogs the next morning, Eli delivered the blow Jonah had feared. Elizabeth, who would spend another day with Violet, was in the house making omelets for breakfast, using the last of the leftover rooster with peas and onions from the garden.

"You know," Eli said, "what we did last night doesn't have to mean anything."

"Hell, no, it doesn't," Jonah said. "That wasn't the first time I've had meaningless sex with a guy. And I can't imagine it will be the last time either."

"I didn't say it was meaningless sex."

"Yes, you did. If sex with me doesn't have any meaning for you, then what can you call it but meaningless sex?"

Jonah kept shoveling feed for the hogs into his pails.

Eli, though, paused in his work and looked at Jonah.

"I'll tell you what," Jonah said. "I'm willing to say it never happened. We'll just deny the whole goddamned thing. We went to bed, promptly fell asleep, and that was that."

"I'm not about to deny what we did. I told you I wanted to do it."

"I'm glad to hear you admit that. But I'll still have to take the blame for hoping it might've meant something to you, and you weren't just another guy looking to get his rocks off. I can't fault you, though. The world is filled with guys like that. My father was one of them. But your father didn't seem to be. Maybe that's why I got my hopes up for you."

Eli put down his shovel. He took the shovel Jonah was using and laid it down next to his. He stood in front of Jonah and looked at him as he had Judge Gideon—with tears in his eyes.

Jonah stared back at him. This man with tears starting to run down his cheeks was last night's confident, smirking asshole sliding his hard naked body between the sheets, taunting Jonah to get into the bed naked himself.

"Okay, Jonah, I apologize for what I said. What we did last night did mean a lot to me. I just wanted you to know you don't have any obligation to consider me your boyfriend. I'm sure there must be a slew of gay guys in Chicago who'd love to do what I did with you last night. You don't have to deny yourself those guys for me."

The squealing hogs on the Daleiden farm would have to wait a bit longer for their feed that morning.

Jonah shamelessly hugged and kissed Eli as the hungry animals watched.

"Can you imagine," Jonah asked, "I might be eager to give up that slew of gay guys in Chicago for you?"

*****

"I hope you can see," Eli said, "I'm a bit confused right now."

He and Jonah had finished their first morning chores together and were on their way to the house for breakfast.

"Not about being gay," Eli continued. "I've always liked men. And then you come along, a damned good-looking openly gay man without a boyfriend. Lucky me."

Jonah stared at Eli.

"It's my mother's situation," Eli said. "That's the most confusing thing of all. She has some secrets she hasn't even told me yet. She faces life in prison for three murders she didn't commit. But how can we be sure the state's attorney doesn't have enough evidence for a jury to convict her? And what do we do if the jury does convict her? Go visit her in prison?"

Jonah shook his head. "We've got to believe in your mother no matter what. You and I have no right to her secrets. Everybody has secrets, and they're entitled to reveal them or not as they see fit. We've got to stand by your mother. We've got to do our work here on your farm—and do whatever else we can—to help her."

Jonah stopped and hugged Eli again.

"I agree with you," Jonah said. "No matter what else happens, we're in this together."

*****

That night, after Jonah shaved and showered, Eli, who'd shaved and showered himself, was waiting for him in the no-man's-land. Jonah didn't have a chance to turn out the light before Eli had his hands all over him.

Other nights followed the same pattern. Even nights Jonah drove back to Chicago, he almost always spent some time with Eli in his bedroom before he left.

*****

"I'm losing you," Frank said.

He was wearing only the skimpy running shorts he favored in the summer.

"You're spending most of your life out there, Jonah. On that farm the wrongly accused widow owns."

Frank sat on Jonah's couch with his legs spread apart as if he were making an attempt to seduce his host, who occupied the leather chair directly across the coffee table. Frank and Jonah, though, were well beyond that.

"Do you have your own bedroom out there?"

"No, I don't."

"Oh, Jesus. You're sleeping in the same bed with that woman's beautiful eighteen-year-old son?"

"That's right. I am."

"Christ, you've done it. You're having sex with him."

"I didn't initiate it. He did. He made the first move. So yeah, we're having sex."

Frank laughed.

"And now you've got the boyfriend you've been looking for. And he's a nice, sweet, farmer boyfriend, too. You win again. As you always do."

"Eli and I aren't boyfriends."

"Oh, Jonah, please. Why are you so fucking reluctant to admit you love this guy?"

"He's only eighteen."

"So what? I wouldn't have to be a lawyer to tell you he's perfectly legal."

"He's legal, but he's too young for me to insist he say he loves me."

"So you can't tell him you love him because then he'd have to tell you he loved you, too?"

"Or not. I'd be forcing him into a corner. I refuse to do that. For now, we're just having sex. It's nothing more. You of all people should be able to understand that."

Chapter Nine

Violet filed a motion asking Gideon to set the earliest possible date for Elizabeth's trial.

The media from Chicago showed up in full force for the hearing. Jill was among them.

Gideon had carefully arranged the seating in the spectators' gallery in his courtroom for Elizabeth's trial and any related proceedings. Those involved in the case such as witnesses and the defendant's family members sat in the first row. Reporters crowded into the next two rows.

Eli, Belle and Jonah sat in the front row behind Elizabeth and Violet. Jill took a seat behind them in the second row.

Violet had Eli sworn in as a witness.

Violet once again led him through an identification of himself as the defendant's eighteen-year-old son, who would begin attending classes at Northern in September.

"Do you also wish to attend your mother's trial in this court?" she asked.

"I'm her son, her only child. I want to be present for every moment of her trial in this court."

Gideon asked Eli the next question.

"Would a trial extending beyond Labor Day cause you to miss classes at Northern?"

"Yes, it would," Eli replied.

Tanner rose from his chair.

"Your Honor," he said, "the People join in the defendant's motion for a trial at the earliest possible date."

Gideon looked at his calendar.

"I'll set the trial of these cases for the first of August. That's a Monday."

He turned to Eli.

"Thank you for your testimony. You're free to go now."

*****

Jonah noticed a black Buick at least ten years old moving slowly toward him.

He was in the garden, which lay north of the road between

Elizabeth's house and the seven oak trees where Henry and Titus's house once stood. He was harvesting the vegetables for the supper he and Eli would have ready when Elizabeth arrived home from Violet's office.

Shielding his eyes from the sun with his hand, he stood up. He realized the driver of the Buick was Olivia.

He'd seen her in the courtroom earlier that week when Gideon granted Violet's request for an early trial. Olivia also had a seat in the front row of the gallery.

She drove her car onto the shoulder of the road and came to a stop. She got out and walked down the rows of the garden approaching Jonah.

"I'm thrilled," she said, "Judge Heidecker set an early date for Elizabeth's trial."

"Why does that please you so much?" Jonah asked.

"Elizabeth should've been sent to prison many years ago. We shouldn't have to wait even until August to see that happen."

Jonah stared at his visitor and chose to make no response.

"Tanner tells me he'll call you to testify at the trial," Olivia said. "And I hope to God when you testify, you tell the truth."

"I can't imagine why you might think I wouldn't."

Olivia laughed, waving her hand in the direction of Elizabeth's house.

"It's obvious," she said, "you've fallen under her spell."

"I like Elizabeth a lot, if that's what you mean."

"Let me warn you. I had a tape recorder with me when I came to see you at your house in Chicago. I've got down every word you said about your conversation with Elizabeth. The man at the store assured me I was buying the best recorder on the market. So if your testimony deviates one iota from what you told me, I'll badger Tanner Howland until he prosecutes you for perjury and has you thrown in prison, too."

"I told you I intend to tell the truth. So I'm not worried about prison for myself. But for an innocent woman, I worry a lot."

"Innocent? How can you use such a word to describe Elizabeth?"

"She's incapable of killing another human being."

Olivia looked at Jonah as if he were a child.

58

"They haven't told you," she said. "I'm not surprised."

"What are you talking about?"

"Even her son won't tell you."

"Tell me what?"

"Those two old neighbors and her father aren't the only people Elizabeth has murdered. Eli can tell you all about her most recent killing. He was there. He watched it happen. And you call her an innocent woman."

Jonah once again remained silent.

"I'll give you another reason for telling the truth, Mr. Neumeyer. I know what you're doing with my grandson. I know why you're living in the same house with Elizabeth and Eli. I've connected the dots. The more simpleminded folks around here haven't done that yet. But I could help them do it."

She laughed at the clever way she'd put matters.

"If you don't tell the truth, I'll let them know you're a queer from Chicago who seduced my eighteen-year-old grandson. Do you imagine even the hayseeds in Concord County won't be able to guess what sort of perverted things you're doing with that sweet, innocent boy?"

"I think it's time for you to leave."

Jonah still thought Elizabeth was incapable of killing another human being. He wasn't so sure, though, about himself.

*****

Elizabeth had news for Eli and Jonah at the supper table in the kitchen that evening.

"Violet received Tanner's list of trial witnesses just before I left today. You're on it, Jonah. So is Olivia."

"I don't understand," Eli said. "What's she got to say about anything?"

"She's one of the reasons," Elizabeth said, "Violet and I have spent so much time together. We've tried to consider all the possibilities. But we're fairly certain now what she'll say. That's why we asked for an early trial."

"So what do you and Violet think she'll say?" Eli asked.

Elizabeth shook her head. "I'm sorry. I can't tell you that."

"I imagine," Jonah said, "Violet has asked you not to reveal the details of your strategy to anyone else. Not even Eli and me. In case we accidentally spill it to other people."

"Violet laid down that rule the day I hired her."

"Wisely," Jonah said.

*****

"Your grandmother told me your mother murdered a fourth person, somebody in addition to her father, Henry and Titus. She told me you know who that person is."

Jonah and Eli had set aside the afternoon to repair the fence enclosing the woods on the slopes on either side of the creek. During spring, summer and early autumn, the hogs roamed the woods. They ate the acorns from the oak trees with as much gusto as they did their usual feed. In late autumn, after the Daleidens finished picking the corn, the hogs roamed the fields searching for and consuming the spilled kernels.

"I know what she's talking about," Eli said, "and it wasn't a murder by a long shot."

"Here," Jonah said, pointing toward a part of the fence he thought needed repair.

Eli was driving the tractor. The hay wagon behind it held the new fencing and the wire cutters and other tools they needed to insert it.

Eli stopped the tractor, jumped down from it and peered at the fence.

"Yeah," he said, "let's replace it all along here."

He pointed toward the corner post where they'd begun their repair job after lunch.

"That should keep us good," he said, "for another two or three years."

"What was your grandmother talking about?"

"Last Christmas."

Jonah looked at Eli. "When your father died?"

"Yeah."

Eli had tears in his eyes.

"Why don't we take a break?" Jonah asked, giving Eli a hug. "I'll run to the house and get us some lemonade. I can use a damned good run."

Eli wiped his face. "I'll come with you."

*****

The run was easy for them since they were both working in gym shorts. They'd decided at lunch the day had gotten too warm and humid for their usual Levi's and tee shirts.

They drank their lemonade at the picnic table on the lawn in the shade of the oaks that grew there. They let the breeze take care of the sweat from their sprint. They faced the garden, the orchard to the north of it, and the dirt path between them that ended at what used to be Henry and Titus's front lawn.

"What happened last Christmas?" Jonah asked.

"On Christmas Eve my mother called some friends and relatives. She let them know she'd agreed with the doctors to remove life support for Dad the day after Christmas. She said if anyone wanted to see my dad alive one last time, they could do it Christmas Day. She got one of Dad's relatives to agree to call my grandmother. After all, Mom told me, Dad was Olivia's son."

"Did your dad want his life support taken away?"

"He told me and my mom three weeks before Christmas that's what he wanted. He could still talk to us then. He was in terrible pain. We hated seeing him like that. He asked me to be brave and pull the plugs myself. Mom wouldn't let me do it, though. She said she'd do it if she could, legally. But no, we had to handle it right and wait for the doctors to decide."

"Where was your father?"

"In the hospital in Oxford. I have to say, the people there were kind to us. They knew what my father wanted. They knew I couldn't do what he asked me to do. They kept an eye on me whenever I was there. They told me if I pulled the plugs, I'd be charged with murdering my own father. I felt helpless. He didn't deserve to suffer like that at the end of his life."

"Did your grandmother show up?" Jonah asked, his arm around Eli's shoulders.

"Yeah, she did. After morning Mass on Christmas Day. She

came right out in front of everybody who was there and accused my mother of wanting to kill my father. She said if Mom told the people at the hospital to turn off Dad's life support, she'd be murdering him."

"You were there? You heard her say that?"

Eli turned to face Jonah.

"I was there all that day. I sat next to my father on his bed. Everybody around here liked him. We had a steady stream of visitors. It was awful. My grandmother accused Mom of wanting to murder Dad just to be done taking care of him. She said Mom couldn't wait for him to die 'a natural death.' Mom pointed to all the tubing attached to Dad. 'You call this a natural life?' she asked."

"You can cry all you want," Jonah said. "You don't need to hide your tears from me."

"My grandmother got loud. Other patients and their visitors complained. The hospital security people came to Dad's room. They tried to calm her down. But she screamed at them for being accomplices to the murder of her son. They told her if she didn't leave, they'd call the police. She left but only to use a pay phone to call the Oxford police herself."

"She called the police?"

"To stop the murder of her son, she said. She ended up calling the chief of the police at his home. He told her the police wouldn't interfere with the doctors. They'd only do that if the state's attorney told them they could. So she called Tanner's office and spoke to the assistant on duty. He told her only the state's attorney himself could help her. She'd have to call back the next day."

"So she let it drop there?"

"Hell, no, she didn't. She was out to stop a murder. She went to see Tanner at his home. He was there with all his children and grandchildren celebrating Christmas. That didn't stop her. He refused to take any action against the hospital. He told her to hire an attorney, file a lawsuit and let a judge decide. So that's just what she did."

"On Christmas Day?"

"She hired the lawyer on Christmas Day. She called the hospital and told Mom she'd given him a substantial check for what she agreed was an extraordinary request. So the first thing the next morning the lawyer would file the suit and get a judge to sign an emergency order to the hospital staff not to shut off Dad's life support. Then Mom and the doctors would have to prove in court she had the legal right to ask them to let Dad die."

"A temporary restraining order. Did the lawyer get one?"

"He did."

"I thought your father died the day after Christmas."

"He did. Mom told the hospital people what my grandmother told her on the phone. Violet came and talked with the doctors. They called their lawyers. They agreed to remove Dad's life support as early as they could the next morning, before the case was filed in court. Mom and I were there when they did it. We were with Dad when they told us he was dead."

Eli picked up the front of his tee shirt to dry his eyes.

"Mom and I came home and did the chores and ate breakfast. My grandmother called later that day. I answered the phone. 'Your mother murdered my son, your father,' she screamed. 'Are you going to take my side, as a good son should? Or will you take your mother's side—and end up in hell with her?'"

"So your grandmother calls the removal of your father's life support a murder? And she wants your mother to pay for that by spending the rest of her life in prison?"

"That's why I never should've gone to my grandmother's fucking birthday party. My mom would've been justified whipping my ass for that."

Chapter Ten

"**I** don't enjoy watching you leave like this."

Eli sat naked on the edge of his bed while Jonah searched the room for his briefs.

"I want to spend every night sleeping beside you," Eli said.

Jonah found his tee shirt and decided to put that on first.

"What am I supposed to do?" he asked. "Move in here?"

"Yeah. That's exactly what I want you to do, Jonah. I don't like sleeping alone in this bed anymore."

Nor did Jonah like sleeping without Eli.

"I told my mother," Eli said, "I'm in love with you."

Jonah, having found his briefs, looked at Eli.

"You told your mother that?"

"She said she already knew. I'd made it all too obvious. She said she was happy for me. She hopes you're in love with me, too."

Jonah sat down on the bed next to Eli and hugged him.

"You know I am," he said.

*****

"Go ahead and laugh," Jonah said. "I admit Eli and I are boy-friends."

"Why would I laugh?" Frank asked.

He was sitting in his shorts on his deck overlooking the garden he and Jonah tended.

"You got that cute eighteen-year-old guy to fall in love with you. I've told you before, Jonah, you're my hero."

The evening was so hot Jonah was down to his running shorts himself.

Frank chuckled. "You're going to testify against his mother in a triple-murder trial. And he still wants to be your lover. Amazing."

"He wants me to move in with him and his mother. He wants us to sleep together every night."

Frank looked at Jonah and grinned.

"Oh, how sweet."

"I guess I'll have to rent out my apartment. I don't know what to do with the furniture. Put it in storage, I guess. I can't take it out there."

"Hell, I've got the answer to that. Leave it right where it is and rent out your apartment furnished."

"And let the tenants wreck it all?"

Frank looked at Jonah and laughed.

"I wouldn't want to see that happen," he said. "All that genuine leather? No, no, no."

Jonah shook his head. He couldn't explain why he wanted to sleep in the same bed with Eli every night, but he did.

Frank took a sip of his gimlet.

"Why don't you let me handle this? I might be able to find a couple of tenants for you. Gay tenants who'd take care of your things."

"Who would they be?"

"You remember the two boyfriends I met from a small town in Iowa?"

"The two you wanted to have a three-way with?"

"That hasn't happened yet."

"Not even the weekend they stayed in your guest bedroom?"

"Not even then. Not even after I wined and dined them, too, the ungrateful bastards."

"Imagine that. They're playing hard to get with Frank Kerrigan, of all people."

"They're moving to Chicago. They've both got jobs lined up beginning in August. They're coming in this weekend to look for an apartment. I showed them yours when they were here. They loved it. They said if they could find an apartment like that and pay the rent I do, they'd be in heaven."

"You knew this was going to happen, didn't you?"

Frank looked at Jonah. "I knew."

"That's why you showed the Iowa guys my apartment."

"That's exactly why."

"Okay, if I rent my apartment to them furnished, what do they do with their own stuff?"

Frank laughed again. "Those two guys? Neither of them owns a stick of furniture. They're still living at home with their parents. They love your leather stuff. And all your paintings of barns and farmhouses—they even like those."

"I'm glad to know they have good taste."

"I'm sure they'll take good care of your stuff. They're both fussy like you. They won't be throwing any wild parties, either."

"They can always walk upstairs for those."

"Precisely. Following in your footsteps, so to speak."

"How old are they?"

"Nineteen."

"They're not going to college?"

"No college for them, they say. Getting through high school was enough."

"Tell them they can have the apartment for the same rent you pay."

"Well, wait a minute. You're renting them your furnishings, too. You've got to charge them for that, Jonah. They thought they'd have to lay out money for furniture. Their families don't have anything to give them. I was thinking of making them a loan."

Jonah took a drink of his wine.

"Do these friends of yours," he asked, "tell you they're too much in love with each other to have sex with anybody else?"

"You've got it. That's the way they talk. So far, at least."

"They can pay what you do. I'll need their phone numbers, though."

"I'll get you those. Are you going to tell them they have to behave themselves?"

"No. I'm going to make it crystal clear to them they don't have to have sex with you in order to get or keep the apartment. I think I need to do that."

Frank laughed. "And I'll be grateful to you for telling them that. When they have sex with me, I'll want them to do it because they think I'm hot. And certainly not because they owe me anything."

"*When* they have sex with you? Shouldn't that be *if* they have sex with you?"

Frank laughed again. "I used the right word, Mr. English Major."

*****

Jonah returned to the farm the next morning in time to have lunch with Eli and Elizabeth.

Violet had chosen that day to organize her notes before she and Elizabeth went through her testimony, including her possible answers on cross-examination by Tanner Howland, one last time before the trial.

When Jonah sat down at the table, Elizabeth looked at him and smiled.

"Eli tells me he's fallen in love with you," she said.

Jonah glanced at Eli. He remembered the first time he saw that delightful smirk in full bloom—the first night they slept together.

Jonah turned back to Elizabeth.

"I think you need to know," he said, "I'm also in love with Eli."

"And I hope you know," she said, "how glad I am to hear that. It means more to me than you might think."

"I have to clear up one thing, though," Jonah said. "It's about our ages."

"We haven't done anything illegal," Eli said. "You told me that yourself."

"Violet told me the same thing," Elizabeth said. "Eli was eighteen. Violet assured me he was old enough. You and he even waited until he was out of high school."

Jonah realized Elizabeth knew the first night he and Eli slept together was also the first time they had sex.

"I guess we can be proud Illinois was the first state to legalize what adults of the same gender might wish to do," she said. "Violet didn't need to explain that to me. But I'm glad we had a talk about it anyway."

"I'm twenty-eight," Jonah said. "I have ten years more experience as a gay man than Eli."

Eli scoffed. "What in hell difference does that make?"

Jonah was going to reply, but he saw Elizabeth lay down her fork and look out the window toward the garden and the orchard and the path between them.

"Henry," she said, "was ten years older than Titus. I never heard it was a problem for them. I'm not at all concerned about your ages."

"Yeah," Eli said, rubbing his leg against Jonah's under the table, "we're done worrying about inconsequential things like that."

Elizabeth smiled at Jonah again.

"Eli also tells me he's asked you to move in with us."

"Yeah," Eli said, "that's what I want to talk about. It's silly for Jonah to live in two places. I want him to live here with us all the time and be a part of our family."

"So do I," Elizabeth said, looking at Jonah. "And I admit I have a selfish reason for it."

"You might have a reason for it," Jonah said, "but I'm sure it's not a selfish one."

Elizabeth sighed. "I haven't told either of you this, but Violet isn't optimistic I'll be acquitted. She thinks any Concord County jury we get will more likely than not find me guilty on all three charges. She assumes it will come down to my testimony—whether the jurors believe me. I'll have to testify. If I don't, she's certain any jury will agree Tanner's case is strong enough to convict me. I want you both to understand this. Even if I do testify, I could go to prison for the rest of my life. And lose this farm and everything we've worked for."

"I understand those things are possible," Eli said, "but I'm not ready to give up on you."

"Nor am I," Jonah said. "Not if the case depends upon your testimony."

"I'm grateful for your support," Elizabeth said. "But I do have to consider I might have to leave Eli alone in the world. I don't want to think about that, but I must. I assume you know if I'm convicted, I'll lose the properties I inherited from my father and Henry and Titus. It's the law, Violet tells me. But at least if Eli is with you, Jonah, facing prison and losing my farm won't be so difficult for me. I'm glad you're twenty-eight. I think your ten years as a gay man are all to the good, for you and Eli."

"No jury will convict you, Mom," Eli said.

"I agree with Eli," Jonah said. "I can't imagine any jury reaching such a decision."

Elizabeth looked at Eli and Jonah and grimaced.

"Violet says we can't be so sure about that. But whatever happens, Jonah, thank you for being so kind to my son. Thank you for loving him. If I have to go to prison, at least I'll know he's safe with you."

Chapter Eleven

The next Saturday Jonah and Eli drove to Chicago to pick up Jonah's clothes and books.

As soon as they got inside Jonah's apartment, Frank came down the back stairs, again wearing nothing but his running shorts.

"I've got the lease and a check for the security deposit," he said.

He handed those documents to Jonah at the door without looking at him, as if his old friend were a butler on Masterpiece Theatre.

Frank made it clear Eli was the person he wished to see. He walked across the room to him and extended his hand.

"I'm pleased to meet you, Eli," he said. "I'm Frank. Jonah has told me so much about you."

Eli shook Frank's hand.

"I saw you on your back deck," Eli said, "the other time I was here. When Jonah and I were leaving. You remember that?"

Frank laughed. "I'll never forget it. I thought the most beautiful young guy in the world had spent the previous night with Jonah. Imagine how goddamned jealous that made me feel."

*****

Frank's nineteen-year-old friends had signed the lease.

Jonah placed it on his kitchen table and took the ballpoint pen Frank handed him.

"I spoke with both of them on the phone," Jonah said, looking at Frank. "They tell me they can handle you. I won't believe that, of course, until I see it."

Frank, appreciating what he considered flattery, laughed again.

"I can't help but notice, though," Jonah said, "they're using a check from you as their security deposit. Some clever lawyer must've advised them how to endorse it over to me."

"It's a loan," Frank said. "They agreed to a repayment schedule."

"I'll bet you used one of your office forms for the folks you sue who finally decide it might be better to pay up than fight you anymore."

"You'll win that bet."

"You could easily cancel their obligation before sex, after getting them high on your homegrown pot. Dramatically, too. You could burn the check and repayment schedule in your fireplace."

Frank looked at Eli. "Do you find Jonah as amusing as I do?"

"If enlightenment is amusing," Eli said, "then I'd say Jonah is the most amusing person I've ever met."

"I'm going to sign the lease," Jonah said. "Your friends didn't convince me they can keep you at bay, but they are in love with the idea of living in this apartment. Who am I to deny them such happiness?"

*****

Frank stayed to help carry Jonah's stuff to the car. And take every opportunity he could to cross Eli's path—and give him, Jonah noticed, that silly grin he came on to guys with.

"So they don't have to guess," he'd told Jonah, "whether I'll say yes."

At one point he stopped Eli to speak about something and stood far too close to him.

Jonah couldn't avert his eyes, but he was too far away to hear what they were saying.

*****

"Frank tried to grope me."

"Yeah," Jonah said, "I saw that."

Jonah and Eli were driving home in time to help Elizabeth with the evening chores.

"You saw that?" Eli asked. "Your best friend did that right in front of you, and you didn't say a word?"

"I knew Frank would do that."

"You knew he'd do it, but you never bothered to warn me?"

"I didn't think it was necessary. You're eighteen now. You know everything there is to know about being gay."

"Oh, come on, Jonah, I never said that."

Jonah shrugged. "Okay, you never said that."

"I've never claimed to be anything more than a stupid farm boy."

"You're not stupid. But anyway, whatever you used to know, you now also know some men are like Frank. And I can assure you a lot

72

of other men appreciate the Franks of this world for being the way they are. They get stoned and take acid and listen to Pink Floyd and have sex all day and night and claim they're in heaven. Who am I to say they aren't?"

Jonah, who was driving, kept his eyes on the Eisenhower Expressway ahead of them.

"I saw Frank's hand fall short of its goal. What did you say to him?"

"I told him I didn't want him to do that. That's when he stopped. Then I told him we couldn't be friends if he did things like that. He said he wanted to be my friend. He said you and I have got to use his guest room whenever we come back to Chicago to visit. He promised he wouldn't try to molest me again."

Jonah laughed. "Well, I'd have to say you handled that perfectly. You could've screamed bloody murder. You could've punched out his lights. You would've been justified doing either of those things. Instead, you were polite but firm. Now why was I supposed to warn you—and not let you go through that excitement on your own?"

Eli chose to stare at the road ahead as well.

"Frank hasn't given up on you," Jonah said. "That was just the first act in his usual drama. He let you know how much he likes you. And he doesn't care how many scenes it takes from here to get him to the final curtain. He'll always dream of the day you'll say yes to him. You'll be such a wonderful prize, too. You're young and hot. And the frosting on your delectable cake will be his success in getting you to cheat on me."

Eli looked at Jonah. "And you don't hate the bastard?"

"No," Jonah said, still staring at the road. "I envy him. Consider what he has to look forward to. You. And forever—if you make him wait that long."

*****

They reached the tollway to Aurora before either Eli or Jonah spoke again.

"I don't blame you," Eli said. "I can see why you fell in love with Frank. He's an attractive man. When did it happen?"

73

"At the end of the Summer of Love, 1967. We were both eighteen. It was our first year in college, at Champaign-Urbana. We met at an antiwar demonstration. He was the first man I had sex with. We moved into a dormitory room together and lived in it, summers included, for the next six and a half years."

Jonah changed his lane to let a driver in a hurry pass him.

"I thought Frank's need for the conquest of other men would someday seem as pointless to him as it did to me. But that never happened."

*****

Jonah and Eli were at the last tollbooth waiting their turn.

"I have a confession to make," Jonah said. "I told the nineteen-year-olds Frank has a key to their apartment. I offered to tell him to give it to them. But they said that won't be necessary. If they accidentally lock themselves out, it'll be convenient for them to use Frank's key."

"So what's your confession?"

"I let those guys have the apartment despite what I could see they're getting themselves into. I was afraid if I turned them down, they'd start crying on me. They really did have their hearts set on it."

Jonah pulled out of the tollbooth.

"I'm damned glad," Eli said, "we're going home to Mom's farm."

Jonah glanced at Eli and smiled.

"So am I," he said.

"Your tenants ought to know by now what they're getting into with Frank. And that's an awfully nice apartment for two nineteen-year-old guys with no savings and minimum wage jobs. You aren't responsible for what happens to them."

"Maybe not. I still told Frank if he breaks them up, he might find out I'm my mother's son."

"What's that supposed to mean?"

"I might kill the asshole."

Eli laughed. "You'd never kill anybody. Especially not Frank. He's the first guy you had sex with, for God's sake."

Eli turned to look at the road ahead of them again. He raised his hand and pointed his finger.

"There's the guy who was tailgating you."

A state police officer had pulled him over.

"Don't laugh when we drive by," Jonah said.

He and Eli both did anyway, and the tailgater saw them do it.

"My grandmother would call that schadenfreude," Jonah said.

"Did she know German?"

"She spoke and read it. She had to. Her parents, my great-grandparents, came to America as adults and never learned to speak or read English."

Chapter Twelve

The first morning of the trial, on Monday, August 1, 1977, Violet, Elizabeth, Eli, Belle and Jonah ascended the courthouse stairs single file in the narrow space the media and deputy sheriffs allowed them.

They declined, though, to answer any of the questions the reporters shouted at them.

Jill had told her viewers Elizabeth Daleiden's case was "the extraordinary story of a farmer's widow charged with committing three murders more than twenty years ago. One of her alleged victims was her own father. The other two were elderly farmers who were believed to be homosexual."

Jill said Elizabeth's neighbors and the people who knew her in Revere consistently used the word "different" to describe her. Years ago, about the time of the alleged murders, she'd refused to give up the high school classmate she'd fallen in love with despite the ardent opposition of his Roman Catholic family. And she wouldn't consider becoming a Catholic herself.

Jill went on to say the neighbors and townspeople told her it was commonly known Elizabeth wasn't a believer in any religion.

"Elizabeth's family has confirmed to me," Jill said, "that Elizabeth never attended church as a child. And when she became an adult, she chose on her own not to belong to any religion or attend religious services of any kind other than weddings or funerals. Daniel Daleiden, the man she married and raised a son with, made that same choice for himself."

Elizabeth and Violet had decided any attempt to deny or cover up her nonbeliever status, no matter what the jurors might think of it, could only, when the truth inevitably came out, make her appear to be a liar.

Eli agreed that strategy was the right one. As did Belle and Jonah.

*****

Gideon, Tanner and Violet used up the first day questioning prospective jurors.

Violet asked each of the men in the jury pool what he thought should be done with people she called "homosexuals." But she didn't ask the women in the pool the same question, and Tanner, who apparently didn't want to deal with the issue yet, declined to ask any such question himself.

Later, Violet objected to the inclusion on the jury of all those men who favored execution, castration, life in a prison or mental institution or electroshock as the proper treatment for gay persons.

When she first raised the objection, Tanner asked Gideon for a sidebar, which was a private conference Tanner, Violet and Gideon accomplished by speaking out of the earshot of everyone except the court reporter they hovered over.

After Violet made one point, Gideon stared at Eli, Jonah and Belle, who again sat in the first row of spectators directly behind Elizabeth.

When Gideon returned to his bench, he announced that he'd exclude from the jury all those in the jury pool Violet could prove, from their own testimony, were homophobic.

As a result, Violet got a jury of ten women and two men. The two alternate jurors were also women.

One of the male jurors worked for a bank in Oxford. He started his employment there, he said, "straight out of college twenty-five years ago." He was married for as many years and had three children and, "already, two grandchildren." He favored what he called the idea of "live and let live" for individuals he referred to as "gay."

The second male juror was a twenty-five-year-old who described himself as a farmer. He and his wife, a graduate from Northern who taught math and science in high school in a small Concord County town, had built a home on his parents' four-hundred-acre farm. He finished high school but said he "never had any interest" in going to college. He was an only child and expected to inherit the farm eventually. He also had no objection to persons he called "gays."

"If a man wants to go to bed with another man," he said, "or a woman with a woman, I can't see why it should make any difference to me."

And Tanner could hardly attempt to block these paragons of civic duty.

The farmer told Gideon he and his wife had scheduled a vacation in August with some friends at Lake Geneva, but they'd agreed to give him up and let him sit on Elizabeth Daleiden's jury—if that's what the judge wanted him to do.

The banker and his entire family were scheduled for a vacation in August in Door County, when and where they'd gone "for at least twenty years now." But they too wouldn't stand in the way of his serving to determine the guilt or innocence of Elizabeth Daleiden.

*****

After Elizabeth, Eli and Jonah did their chores that evening, they drove back to Oxford to enjoy a meal Belle had prepared for them and Violet.

"I'd love to find out," Jonah said to Violet at the supper table, "what you, Tanner and Gideon said in your sidebar."

Violet looked at Jonah and smiled.

"You know I can't tell you what we said, not until the trial is over."

"I certainly wouldn't expect you to tell us until the trial is over. I suppose, on the other hand, we're free to speculate on the nature of your conversation."

Violet laughed. "You'd be exercising nothing less than your First Amendment right to free speech."

Belle looked at Jonah. "Do you intend to speculate?"

"If you wish," Jonah replied. "I imagine the state's attorney took issue with the defendant's attorney objecting to prospective jurors based on their views regarding homosexual persons. After all, the defendant isn't claiming she's such a person. Two of the alleged victims might've been. But how is their homosexuality a concern of a defendant who'd pled not guilty to murdering them?"

"And then?" Violet asked.

"I assume," Jonah replied, "the defendant's attorney somehow informed the judge that other individuals associated with the defendant are such persons, and that could very well come out at the trial."

It was Belle's turn to laugh.

"I wonder who those individuals might be."

She and Violet had always described themselves, even to

members of their families, as "best friends." She'd said she was prepared for that to change. If, as a result, she and Violet needed to leave Concord County, she'd sell the bookstore and start over somewhere else.

"And the judge," Jonah said, remembering his look, "ruled in favor of the defendant."

"Gideon," Elizabeth said, "played basketball for Oxford High at the same time Daniel played for Revere High. When they played against one another, they referred to themselves as 'friendly rivals.'"

"Weren't they also," Eli asked his mother, "friendly rivals for your attention?"

Elizabeth looked at her son as if his eighteen-year-old impertinence pleased her.

"I was aware," she replied, "the high school boy who became Judge Heidecker possibly envied my attention to your father."

Belle glanced at Jonah as if she were Holmes and he Watson.

"Maybe that would explain," she said, turning to Elizabeth, "why Judge Heidecker seems so fatherly whenever the witness is your son."

Violet also looked at Jonah.

"Would you say Judge Heidecker's possible youthful envy regarding Elizabeth is something Tanner Howland needs to know about? In case he might wish to ask Judge Heidecker to let another judge hear Elizabeth's case?"

"No, I wouldn't," Jonah replied. "Only if Judge Heidecker, whose possible envy it was—or wasn't—himself believes Tanner needs to know that. So far, I take it, he's decided Tanner doesn't need to hear about a high school boy's infatuation almost thirty years ago—if it existed at all."

*****

"How did you find out Judge Heidecker was your father's rival for your mother?"

It was the first thing Jonah asked Eli when they were alone again in their bedroom.

"My mother told me he was. It was the day Violet learned he

80

was the judge assigned to hear my mother's case."

"You and your mother speak frankly on these subjects?"

"We do."

"She seems to know the first time you had sex with anybody was with me. And it happened the first night you and I slept in this bed together."

"Why shouldn't she know that, Jonah? Why wouldn't I tell her? She is my mother. I am her son."

"Your mother knew you were gay when I was still worried about going to bed with you?"

"Of course she knew."

"Your mother knew, but I didn't."

"I wanted it to be a surprise for you. I thought it would be more fun that way. And it was. I got to seduce you."

"You were taking a chance I might not wish to have sex with you."

Eli finished removing his clothes.

"I'm sorry, Jonah, but I honestly didn't think I was taking much of a chance. You never tried to grope me the way Frank did. You're too much of a gentleman for that sort of thing. But you always seemed pleased when we were together. Even that day I went to Chicago to let you know how pissed I was, and I told you everything was all your fault."

Eli lay down on his side of the bed.

"Whatever happened to our no-man's-land?" he asked.

Jonah, sliding between the sheets himself, ignored Eli's question. He had one of his own.

"Did your father know you were gay?"

"He did."

"Was he as okay with it as your mother is?"

"Oh, yeah. They both just wanted me to find somebody to be happy with. The way they were with each other."

"You think he wouldn't mind knowing his son was in this house having sex with another man?"

"Hell, no, he wouldn't. Especially if he knew the other man was you. He liked you as much as Mom did. You were the boy down the road who fired his grandmother's hired man and did the work himself. They loved that story."

Chapter Thirteen

On Tuesday, August 2, Tanner began the second day of the trial by asking Gideon to admit into evidence three death certificates.

Violet, seated at the counsel table with Elizabeth, rose and said the defendant had no objection to the admission of the documents.

Gideon silently read the three documents.

"I'll admit these," he said and turned to the jury. "The first is the death certificate for Jacob Reifert. It shows the date of his death as May 25, 1950. It gives the cause of his death as 'lethal alcohol intoxication, accidental.'"

Violet rose again. "The defendant will stipulate that Jacob Reifert was her father."

"Thank you," Gideon said and turned to the jury again. "The other certificates show that Henry Hassenauer and Titus Peltz were pronounced dead on December 17, 1955. The cause of both of their deaths is given as 'home fire, smoke inhalation, lethal burns, accidental.'"

Violet had remained standing.

"The defendant will further stipulate," she said, "that Henry Hassenauer and Titus Peltz were her closest neighbors."

*****

Tanner's first witness was Colby Smith, who testified he was seventy-three and retired.

He was one of the two grand jury witnesses on Tanner's list whose names neither Elizabeth nor Violet had initially recognized. But by the time Elizabeth saw him take a seat in the first row of spectators at the bail bond hearing, she was certain who he was. She and Violet assured Eli, Belle and Jonah they knew why he'd testify at the trial.

"Were you employed on May 25, 1950?" Tanner asked Colby.

"I was."

"Who did you work for?"

"Royal Glendenning. He was the Concord County sheriff back then. I was a deputy sheriff."

Colby didn't look at Tanner during his questioning. He stared at Elizabeth instead.

"Were you on duty on Thursday, May 25, 1950?"

"I was."

"Did anything unusual involving yourself happen during your work hours that day?"

"You better believe something unusual happened that day."

Jonah knew Violet could've asked to have the answer stricken in favor of a simple yes or no. Instead, she remained silent.

"What happened?" Tanner asked.

"Another deputy and I were sent to Jacob Reifert's farm in Revere Township."

"Do you know why you and the other deputy were sent to Jacob Reifert's farm in Revere Township on May 25, 1950?"

"As I understood it, his daughter, the defendant, had called the sheriff's office. She said she'd come home from school that afternoon and found her father in his bed. She claimed she couldn't wake him up, he wasn't breathing, and he had no pulse."

From "as I understood it" forward, Jonah knew the answer was inadmissible conjecture. But Violet remained silent again. The answer was also probably, graphically true.

"Did you and the other deputy arrive at the Reifert residence?"

"Yes, sir, we did."

"What did you find when you got there?"

"The daughter, the defendant, let us in. She told us only she and her father lived there. Her mother had died a long time ago. She had no sisters or brothers. She took us to her father's bedroom. She was right. Her father was dead as a doornail. He wasn't breathing. He had no pulse. He was staring at the ceiling with his eyes wide open."

"What did you and the other deputy do then?" Tanner asked.

"We called the office in Oxford here. We spoke to the sheriff himself. He told us to prepare a report and bring the body to the morgue. The coroner would take it from there."

"Did you prepare a report?"

"I didn't. The other deputy did. He signed it, too. I didn't."

One of Tanner's two assistants got up from her chair at the counsel table and handed him a document. She'd also graduated from the University of Illinois Law School in the class of 1974 with Jonah, Frank and Jill.

Tanner showed the document to Colby, who finally had to take his eyes off Elizabeth.

"Have you seen this before?"

Colby scoffed. "Yeah, I've seen that before."

"Can you tell us what it is?"

"Sure. That's the report the other deputy wrote up and signed when we were at the Reifert residence the day Jacob died. You can see I didn't sign it."

"Why didn't you sign it?"

"Because it's bullshit."

Gideon picked up his gavel and slammed it down even before he heard the first titters from the packed courtroom, some of them coming from the television and newspaper reporters, some even from the jurors.

"Mr. Smith," Gideon said as the nascent laughter died, "this is a court of law. I don't allow language like that. I'm ordering your last remark stricken. Please restate your answer to Mr. Howland's question."

"I'm sorry, Your Honor," Colby said as his eyes returned to Elizabeth. "It won't happen again. I refused to sign that document. It says the same thing Jacob Reifert's death certificate says. He died of some kind of accidental alcohol intoxication. Those were the words the sheriff said we should use. I told him I didn't want to sign the report. He said I didn't have to sign it. The other deputy would. If I wanted to keep my job, I should just shut up and help him bring the body to the morgue. That's all I needed to do."

Tanner and Gideon paused, waiting for Violet's objection.

What the sheriff said was hearsay. But Violet had chosen to let former deputy Colby Smith tell his story without any interruption from her. She remained silent once again.

"Why, specifically," Tanner asked his witness, "didn't you want to sign the report?"

"Everything in that bedroom was suspicious," Colby replied. "There were signs of a struggle. Jake's sheets were all tangled. The lamp on the table next to the bed had been knocked over. It was lying on the floor, broken in pieces. Jake's face looked funny, bruised a bit I'd have to say, as if he'd been suffocated with his own pillow."

Tanner had made no attempt to establish Colby's credentials as an expert witness who could testify as to the appearance of a suffocated corpse, let alone one killed by a fiend using the victim's own pillow.

Still, Violet declined to object.

"Did you question Jacob's daughter, now the defendant in this courtroom, about what you saw?"

"I did, but she had explanations for everything. Jake's sheets were always tangled, she said. The alcohol he drank made him toss and turn, she told us. The lamp in pieces on the floor wasn't the first one Jake had knocked over getting into bed drunk. And her father's face looked the same to her as it always did. She even said something about me never seeing Jake outside a dimly lit bar before. So how could I tell if her father looked any different than he usually did in daylight? That's how sassy she was, speaking to deputy sheriffs. She never shed a tear, either."

Colby had his eyes fixed on Elizabeth, but no more so than she had hers on him.

"But the sheriff told me just to forget about it. I knew what the real problem was. He already had too much on his hands that day. He didn't want to be told, in addition, some eighteen-year-old girl, about to graduate from high school, had killed her alcoholic dad. But she could've done it. I was much younger then—that was twenty-seven years ago—but I never would've picked a fight with her. You could tell she did farmwork. She was perfectly capable of suffocating her father with his pillow. Hell, she still looks as if she could do it today."

Violet even declined to object to any of that.

"Oh, no," Colby offered, without being asked, "something far more important than Jake Reifert's death happened that day in Revere Township. The sheriff had reporters in his office shoving microphones in his face."

Jonah knew why.

And Tanner saw no reason not to ask the obvious question.

"What else happened that day in Revere Township?"

"The eighteen-year-old Neumeyer girl shot and killed her eighteen-year-old boyfriend when he refused to marry her. She used her father's shotgun. Then, when the deputies came to pick her up and take her to jail, she shot and killed herself. It was a huge story that day. Even the newspapers and stations in Chicago sent reporters. The Neumeyer girl and her boyfriend had a one-year-old son. I'm told he lived with his grandparents after that. I'm also told he's in court today. He'd be twenty-eight years old now. I understand he's got some connection to this case."

Colby's eyes wandered to the people sitting in the first row behind Elizabeth.

When Colby's gaze reached him, Jonah nodded, letting him know he'd found his man.

*****

Jonah could see the juror in the middle of the first of the two rows of jurors and alternates was taking notes of Colby's testimony. He remembered she'd said she taught grade school in Oxford, and she, too, was willing to forgo a planned family vacation to serve on Elizabeth Daleiden's jury.

*****

Violet remained seated during her cross-examination of Colby Smith.

"Mr. Smith, did you personally know Jacob Reifert?"

"I did. Jake and I drank in King Arthur's Inn, the bar in Oxford. Elizabeth was right about that. I never saw him in daylight. Hell, I never knew him as Jacob. That's what we were supposed to call him in the report. That's what Tanner and his people call him. But he was Jake to me. Anyway, the town of Revere had just that one dinky bar. Still has. Same name, too: 'The Ride Inn.' The patrons there took a dislike to Jake for some reason. The owner threw him out one night three or four years before he died—or got murdered. He had a reputation as a guy who liked to pick fights. After he came up to Oxford and started drinking with us, though, I never heard he started a fight. He was in a strange situation with his daughter, the defendant in this case. He'd tell us about it sometimes when he was drunk."

"What did Jake tell you?" Violet asked.

"His daughter was still in high school then, but she was the one who gave him his drinking money. In fact, she doled out all the money he ever saw. She bought his groceries. She did a lot of the work on the farm. She was the boss. Two elderly brothers who were their nearest neighbors helped her. Jake didn't have much of a say in things. He had to take what his daughter gave him. And she was still in high school. It was the strangest damned story I'd ever heard."

Tanner didn't appear to be pleased with his witness's revelations on cross-examination.

Jonah suspected Tanner's preparation of Smith hadn't taken them this far.

"Mr. Smith," Violet asked, "did Jacob Reifert, or Jake as you knew him, drive to the bar in Oxford and home again after drinking?"

Colby scoffed. "God no. Years before that, he'd caused a terrible accident. He was drunk. Several people died. He lost his license. Once after the accident he bought a cheap used car. But his neighbors wouldn't let him drive it. They'd call the sheriff as soon as they saw him leave his property in it. Most of the time he couldn't even get to Revere, which was only two miles away, before a deputy would pull him over. Then, during his last stay in the county jail, somebody stole that car, or got rid of it, and it was never seen again. By the time I knew Jake, his daughter—the defendant in this case—wouldn't consider giving him the money to buy another car. She was the boss, the one who decided how the money was spent. Jake had no say at all."

Colby briefly glanced at Violet, who remained silent.

"Getting back to your question," Colby said, "another regular from Revere who didn't drink much but liked to talk a lot gave Jake a lift whenever he wanted one. That's how Jake got back and forth to Oxford. Jake didn't seem to mind hearing that man going on about nothing."

"Mr. Smith," Violet asked, "do you still drink?"

"No, I've been in AA the past fifteen years. Jacob should've been in it, too. He might still be alive today. He could've fought off whoever suffocated him with his own pillow."

"Congratulations, Mr. Smith, on your fifteen years with AA," Violet said. "And thank you for your testimony. All of it. Elizabeth and I are both glad you testified today."

Violet turned to Gideon. "I have no further questions for this witness."

*****

"Did an eighteen-year-old farmer's daughter kill her own father?" Jill asked on the news that evening. "A former deputy sheriff's explosive testimony strongly suggests she did."

Jill and her colleagues had interviewed Colby Smith, the former deputy sheriff, at length on the courthouse steps after his testimony that day.

"That Elizabeth Daleiden," he offered at one point, "is one smart cookie."

*****

Elizabeth, Eli and Jonah said little at their supper table after they did their chores.

"Did you know," Jonah asked Elizabeth, "Violet could've made any number of objections to Colby Smith's testimony?"

"She told me that," Elizabeth replied.

"But she didn't object once."

Elizabeth looked at Jonah and smiled. "That's because Colby was telling the truth."

Eli laid down his fork and wiped his mouth with his napkin.

"Mom, please. That weird man—he kept staring at you—was telling the truth?"

Elizabeth turned to Eli and took his hand.

"Violet warned me this wouldn't be an easy case for us to win. It would be even worse if we made the jury think we were attempting to keep Colby from telling them his full story."

"And he told the truth?" Jonah asked.

"Yes," Elizabeth said, "he did. As he saw it. He's an honest man."

Chapter Fourteen

On Wednesday, August 3, Tanner called his second witness, Clyde Lewis, another retired deputy sheriff. He was seventy-five.

He was also the second grand jury witness whose identity had initially been a mystery to Elizabeth and Violet.

"Were you still employed as a deputy sheriff on December 17, 1955?" Tanner asked.

"I was."

"Were you in this courtroom yesterday when Colby Smith testified?"

"Yes, I was."

"And you heard his testimony?"

"Yes, I did."

"Was the Concord County sheriff you worked for in 1955 the same person Colby Smith worked for in 1950?"

"Yes, that was the same man, Royal Glendenning. He'd been the sheriff forever. He won election after election. The voters loved him."

Tanner glared at his own witness.

"Is the person who was the Concord County sheriff in 1950 and 1955 still alive today?"

"No, Royal was pretty old then. He's been dead many years now."

As soon as Clyde was sworn in as a witness, he began staring at a man seated in the first row of spectators. He'd been there the previous two days and during the two pretrial hearings as well. He was the dead sheriff's grandson, Warren Glendenning. He'd graduated in the same law school class with Violet.

The current Republican congressman had announced his retirement at the end of his present two-year term. Warren would be Tanner's opponent in the primary election on March 21, 1978. The race was considered a toss-up. Whoever won would surely also win in November.

The Glendennings were Taft, Goldwater and Reagan Republicans. The Howlands were Eisenhower, Rockefeller and Ford Republicans. Elizabeth Daleiden, the Concord County "farmer's widow" on trial for three murders, was a pawn.

"Were you on duty on Saturday, December 17, 1955?" Tanner

asked Clyde.

"I was."

"Did anything unusual involving yourself happen during your work hours that day?"

"Yeah, I'd say it was awfully unusual."

"What happened?"

"I was sent to Revere Township that night with three other deputies. A farmhouse was on fire. Two old gentlemen lived in it. They'd told people they were brothers, but it turned out they weren't. Anyway, the neighbors believed they were still in the house, even as it burned."

Repeating her strategy from the previous day with Colby, Violet made no objection to Clyde's telling the story as he wished to tell it, even if he was answering questions he'd never been asked.

"What did you do when you reached the scene of the fire?" Tanner asked.

"My three men and I—I was in charge that night—went into the house as soon as we thought it was safe to do so. The defendant and her husband, who were the nearest neighbors of the old men, knew the house. They were volunteer firemen, too. Both him and her. They led the way."

Six-year-old Jonah and his grandmother had watched Elizabeth and Daniel Daleiden go into the house with the deputies. Jonah's grandmother had to hold him back.

"After you were inside the house, did you take any notes on what you observed?"

"I did, even though it slowed us down. One of the deputies had to hold a flashlight for me. That left only the two others to look for evidence about what happened. But I did what I was supposed to do anyway. I wrote more than ten pages of notes."

Jonah remembered the flashlights. He and the other bystanders could see into the house through a living room wall almost completely burned away. For a long while, the deputies pointed their flashlights at the two men who lived in the house, still sitting in their chairs in front of their fireplace. By then, the crowd agreed, they had to be dead.

"What did you do with those notes?" Tanner asked Clyde.

"When I got back to Oxford here, I showed them to Sheriff

Glendenning in his office. He took them. He read them. But he wouldn't give them back to me."

As Colby the previous day couldn't take his eyes off Elizabeth, so Clyde couldn't take his off Warren Glendenning.

"Did Sheriff Glendenning tell you why he wouldn't give the notes back to you?"

"Yes, he did."

"What was his reason?"

"He said my notes made it look as if the two old men had been murdered."

"Did Sheriff Glendenning tell you what he saw wrong with that?"

"He did. He said it would invite controversy. It would make the good citizens of Concord County look bad. People would believe somebody, or maybe even a group of people—a 'mob,' he said—killed the old boys because they were queer."

"Mr. Lewis," Gideon said, without a moment's hesitation, "I'd prefer you not use that word in my courtroom. The word I assume you meant is homosexual or gay. Am I right?"

Clyde's embarrassment seemed to amuse Warren.

"Yes, Your Honor," Clyde said, sneering back at Warren, "that's what I meant."

"Thank you, Mr. Lewis."

Elizabeth turned around in her chair and gave Eli and Jonah a smile, almost as if she'd already won her case.

*****

At Belle's supper on Monday evening, Violet told their guests— Elizabeth, Eli and Jonah—the chief judge of the circuit court hadn't randomly selected Gideon Heidecker to hear Elizabeth's case.

All the other judges in the circuit had ties to either the Howlands or the Glendennings. None of them wanted to decide a legal issue against the side of the people who'd made him a judge. But none of them wished to appear to be a dupe either, especially not with reporters from Chicago, and God only knew where else, looking on.

"They're quite grateful," Violet said, "Gideon is available to handle the hot potato Tanner baked when he convinced a grand jury to indict Elizabeth."

*****

"Did Sheriff Glendenning tell you," Tanner asked Clyde, "why your notes indicated Henry Hassenauer and Titus Peltz had been murdered?"

"Yes, he did. He gave me two reasons. He wasn't stupid. He was right on both points."

"What was his first reason?"

"The old men were still sitting in their chairs when we found them."

Exactly, Jonah agreed. He'd seen them himself.

"If they'd been alive when the fire began," Clyde continued, "they would've gotten up from their chairs and tried to put it out. Elizabeth told us herself they weren't too frail to fight a fire. If their efforts were futile, and the fire overwhelmed them, we would've found them fallen on the floor. Only if they were already dead, or dying, when the fire began would they still be sitting in their chairs."

*****

"What was Sheriff Glendenning's second reason?"

"The rat poison. My deputies went into the kitchen. It wasn't burnt as bad as the rest of the house. One of them beamed his flashlight on a garbage pail filled with empty cans and bottles that would someday end up in the county dump. They found an empty rat poison container on top of the trash. The poison had strychnine in it. I read that on the label. I wrote in my notes, maybe somebody put it in their food, watched them die and then started a fire. But the sheriff was worried people might think somebody broke into the old men's house. It might've been more than one person. Then he used that word again. It might've been a mob. They might've forced the old homosexual men—or whatever they're called now—to eat the rat poison. They might've watched them die and then started the fire to cover up what they did. That's what Sheriff Glendenning was worried about. He told me so himself."

The mob the sheriff envisioned could've been the people Jonah saw and heard at the fire. But Jonah hadn't considered they might've used rat poison to kill Henry and Titus, not when a gun or a knife would've done the job more easily and quickly. Maybe, though, the leaders of the mob were cunning to a degree he hadn't imagined. Despite the extensive burns on the bodies of the victims, the deputies might've been able to detect gunshot or knife wounds.

"Did you have any conversation with Elizabeth Daleiden about who prepared meals for the two old fellows?"

That was a leading question from beginning to end, but Violet made no objection to it.

"I most certainly did," Clyde said. "And I put that in my notes. Elizabeth told me she fixed most of their meals. She cleverly denied, though, preparing any food for them that day. I also put that in my notes."

Tanner allowed himself a brief glance at Warren in the front row before he asked Clyde his next question.

"What happened to the empty rat poison container your deputies found in the old men's kitchen?"

"Sheriff Royal Glendenning took it with my notes. He later told me I could rest assured he'd destroyed everything, my notes as well as the empty rat poison container. He was most grateful, he told me, I'd kept my mouth shut."

Clyde looked at Warren as if he were on trial for murder.

"Of course," Clyde added, "I had a family to feed. I wasn't a rich lawyer or politician."

*****

That day on the courthouse steps the media showered their attention on Clyde Lewis.

But the camera people also caught Elizabeth, Eli, Violet, Belle and Jonah coming down the stairs and stopping their descent when Jill approached them.

"Violet Sutherland," she asked, "why haven't you made a single objection to any of the testimony of the state's attorney's witnesses?"

Violet smiled at Jill.

"My client Elizabeth and I haven't found any of their testimony objectionable. We're glad Mr. Smith and Mr. Lewis have both had a chance to tell their stories in court in full."

"Were they telling the truth?" Jill asked.

"The jury will decide that," Violet said.

"We have to go now," Eli said. "We have work to do. We have a farm to take care of."

Jill looked at Jonah, as if for help.

Jonah merely shrugged.

The reporters made way for them.

"Another former Concord County deputy sheriff," Jill told her viewers that evening from the courthouse steps, "believes he's shown the jury how and why Elizabeth Daleiden got away with murder—this time, two extremely grisly murders of her neighbors."

*****

Eli waited through the drive home, the evening chores and supper preparations before he asked his question. He was at the kitchen table eating the meal with Elizabeth and Jonah.

"Am I also supposed to believe this Clyde Lewis, like Colby Smith, told the truth?"

Elizabeth put down her fork and looked at Eli.

"Clyde told the truth today," she said.

"I know Clyde told the truth about one thing," Jonah said. "I saw what he saw the night of the fire. After the volunteers put it out, Henry and Titus were still sitting in their chairs. It isn't possible they made any effort to fight the fire."

"Clyde was right about that," Elizabeth agreed. "He was also right about the empty rat poison container. One of the deputies found it where Clyde said he did. It was reasonable for him to think it could've had a great deal to do with the deaths of Henry and Titus. The sheriff should've preserved it as evidence. Even Clyde's speculation that I might've killed Henry and Titus myself was justified."

"I think I see what you and Violet are doing," Jonah said. "The other witnesses are telling the jury what you've assumed they would. That's why you spent those hours together. You've figured out you have no reason to object to anything they say. You know, for the jurors, the case will come down to what you tell them. Down to whether they believe you or not. You're convinced they will. Simply because what you'll tell them will complete the story. And the jurors will know it when they hear it."

Elizabeth smiled at Jonah. "I'm awfully glad Eli fell in love with you."

She turned to Eli and shook her head.

"I'm very sorry I can only tell you the story as I tell it to the judge, the jury and the world. I promise you you'll hear the whole story in the next few days. You and Jonah don't have much longer to wait now."

"I don't care how long I have to wait," Jonah said. "I've come up with several ideas about what actually happened on May 25, 1950, and December 17, 1955. In none of them do I imagine you murdered anybody."

Chapter Fifteen

On Thursday, August 4, Tanner called Jonah as his third witness. Tanner soon got to the details of Jonah's conversation with Elizabeth when he went to see her on his birthday in April.

Yes, she'd told him she was certain no intruders, and no mob, had murdered her two neighbors, Henry and Titus.

Tanner could've left the matter there. Former sheriff's deputy Clyde Lewis had provided convincing evidence that the men had been murdered, probably poisoned. So if Elizabeth told Jonah the truth and no intruder or mob did it, who did? She must've known by then the men were leaving their farm to her.

But Tanner wanted to get more out of Jonah than that.

"Is it possible from what Elizabeth told you," Tanner asked, "she could've put rat poison in their food?"

"That's possible for anyone who prepares another person's food. Elizabeth has told me she prepared meals for Henry and Titus. That's what she told Mr. Lewis. I expect she'll tell the jury that herself. But I can't imagine she'd put rat poison in their food. She—"

Tanner wouldn't let Jonah continue.

"I move to strike that last part of Mr. Neumeyer's answer," he said. "'But I can't imagine she'd put rat poison in their food.' It went beyond the scope of my question."

Gideon looked at Tanner as a parent would a disappointing child.

"I can't see how it did, Mr. Howland," he said. "You asked for Mr. Neumeyer's opinion on direct examination. I heard no objection from the defendant's attorney, although she obviously could've made one. So I let your question stand. Mr. Neumeyer has told you why he thinks it might've been possible for the defendant to put poison in her neighbors' food. And now he's telling you why he thinks it wasn't possible for her to do that. Your motion to strike the testimony of your own witness, Mr. Howland, is denied."

Gideon turned to Jonah.

"I don't believe you finished your testimony, Mr. Neumeyer. You may continue."

"Elizabeth didn't put rat poison in their food. She loved those men. After her mother died, they became more like fathers to her than her own father. Well before she reached her teens, the three of them were doing all the work on both farms. They put in long hours together. When Daniel Daleiden came to live with Elizabeth after he and she finished high school, they and Henry and Titus continued to work the two farms together. No, it isn't possible Elizabeth poisoned them."

Tanner, glaring at Jonah, sat down.

"I have no more questions for this witness," he said.

*****

Jonah knew from the look on Olivia's face his testimony would earn him the punishment she'd promised. She'd let the world know what he was—a sodomite indecently taking advantage of her eighteen-year-old grandson, a predator feasting on his innocent prey.

And the godless Elizabeth, of course, was letting him get away with it.

*****

"You may cross-examine the witness, Ms. Sutherland," Gideon said.

Violet once again remained seated during her cross-examination.

"Mr. Neumeyer," Violet said, "you testified on direct examination that you're a lawyer."

"Yes."

"Did you recently practice law in Chicago?"

"Yes, I did."

"Did you recently reside in Chicago?"

"Yes."

"Do you currently practice law?"

"No."

"Where do you currently reside?"

"With the defendant Elizabeth Daleiden and her son Eli. In their farmhouse in Revere Township."

Those remarks brought titters from more than a few of the reporters in the gallery.

Tanner viewed his third witness with a curled upper lip.

"Do you currently work?" Violet asked.

"Yes."

"What kind of work do you do?"

"I do farmwork and housework for the people I live with, Elizabeth and Eli."

"You grew up on a farm in Revere Township, did you not?"

"I did."

"Do the Daleidens pay you for your work?"

"You could say they pay me room and board. But we don't view it that way."

"How do you and the Daleidens view it, Mr. Neumeyer?"

Jonah first looked at Elizabeth and then at Eli sitting directly behind her in the first row of spectators.

"We view it for what it is," Jonah said. "I'm a member of their family."

Violet paused to look at the jury. Then, perhaps having satisfied herself the jurors had heard those remarks correctly, she turned to Jonah again.

"Mr. Neumeyer, did you hear Judge Heidecker's instructions to a previous witness on the use of the word gay in this courtroom?"

"Yes, I did."

"Mr. Neumeyer, do you consider yourself to be gay?"

This time the titters in the gallery rose to such a level that Gideon felt the need to use his gavel to silence them.

"I'm gay," Jonah replied. "And I'm also glad I'm gay."

Tanner could've objected to Jonah's "I'm also glad I'm gay" elaboration, but he didn't.

"Mr. Neumeyer," Violet asked, "why did you pay a visit to the defendant last April?"

"I thought she had information I wanted."

"Information regarding what?"

"The deaths of her neighbors, Henry and Titus. And the fire that destroyed their house. I was at the fire with my grandmother. I was six years old."

Since Tanner didn't object to any of that, Jonah decided to move on.

"I wanted to know if Elizabeth Daleiden could help me discover who murdered the men and set their house on fire."

Violet, glancing at Tanner, decided to move on herself.

"Did you have, Mr. Neumeyer, a preconceived idea of how the men died and their house was set on fire?"

"Yes, I did. I assumed some intruders—very likely more than one person—got into their house and killed them. Then they set the house on fire for good measure. That drew a mob of people who loudly praised the killing of two men they called 'queers,' 'faggots' and 'sodomites.' I was there. I heard them use those terms. But Henry and Titus were just the same as I am: gay. I don't think I deserve to be killed for being who I am. I'm certain the world can remain in good working order no matter whom I love."

"If you'd gotten the information you wanted from Elizabeth, what would you have done with it?"

Jonah looked at Jill, who was still sitting in the second row behind Eli as if she owned the position.

"I would've given the information to the newspapers and the television stations. I would've expected them to help me expose what passed for justice in 1955 in Concord County. Where the authorities made no attempt to find out what really happened to two elderly men after their neighbors learned they weren't the brothers they'd claimed to be."

Before Jonah gave his answer, he'd assumed Tanner wouldn't wish to object to any of it. One of those Concord County authorities in 1955 was the grandfather of his first-row rival, Warren Glendenning.

Tanner remained seated and silent.

*****

After court that day, the media people made it difficult for Elizabeth, Violet, Eli, Belle and Jonah to descend the courthouse steps.

"We only want to go home now," Elizabeth said. "We have livestock to feed and tend to on our farm. We consider it our duty to take good care of them."

"Eli," Jill asked, "how would you describe your relationship with Jonah?"

Eli looked at Jonah. Whatever he said would go out to the world. "I love Jonah," he replied.

"And I love Eli," Jonah said.

"We sleep together in the same bed every night," Eli chose to add.

Jonah gave Eli a hug he knew would appear on television that evening and on the front pages of newspapers the next morning.

"Elizabeth," Jill asked, "do you approve of your son's relationship with Jonah?"

Elizabeth looked at Eli and Jonah and smiled.

"My son's relationship with Jonah doesn't need my approval," she said. "I'll tell you how I feel about them, though. I used to have one son I loved with all my heart. Now I have two."

Chapter Sixteen

Eli drove his mother's car home from Oxford. The events of the day had once again reduced him and his passengers, Elizabeth and Jonah, to silence.

Approaching the Daleiden farm, they saw three Concord County sheriff's cars parked in the driveway but with enough room for another car to pass them. A deputy stood next to each of the first two cars in the line. The current Concord County sheriff, Darrell Glendenning, Warren's cousin and another grandson of Royal Glendenning, stood next to the third.

Jonah could see Judge Gideon Heidecker wasn't the only Concord County luminary who worked out and ran or biked on a regular basis. Darrell's uniform fit him just right. He was another older man Frank would bring home and gloat over when he showed him off to Jonah the next morning.

Darrell motioned for Eli to stop.

Elizabeth, who was in the front passenger seat and nearest the sheriff, had her window down.

"I hope you folks realize," Darrell said, looking inside the car at Jonah and Eli, "you've forced me to do this."

"Darrell," Elizabeth asked, with a familiarity Jonah hadn't expected, "what on earth have we forced you to do?"

"I'm posting two deputies here for as long as it takes."

"Why do you need to do that?" Elizabeth asked. "We aren't breaking any laws here."

Darrell glanced at Eli and Jonah again.

"I've been advised you're not breaking any laws—in this state, at least."

"For the last fifteen years," Elizabeth said.

"I'm aware of that, Elizabeth."

"What's the purpose of posting your deputies here?" Jonah asked.

Darrell looked at Jonah, who was sitting in the backseat behind Elizabeth.

"To keep you alive. You, especially. You're the one the callers threaten the most."

He turned his attention to Elizabeth and Eli.

"We're here to keep all of you alive. Untouched. Safe. Those television and newspaper people from Chicago and New York would love it if some dumb asshole out here in Concord County burned down your house with you folks still inside it. But I won't let that happen."

Darrell stepped back from the car.

"Now go about your business," he said, "as if my people aren't here. I know you farmers have got your chores to do."

He motioned for Eli to continue along the driveway to the garage.

*****

At the supper table that evening Elizabeth told Eli and Jonah she knew Darrell from their high school days. He was a year older than her and Daniel. He played on the Oxford basketball team with Gideon. But she couldn't recall ever speaking at length with him.

"Daniel told me Darrell offered to marry your mother, Jonah, when she was pregnant with you. He made his offer at least once again after you were born."

Jonah had never heard this part of his mother's story.

"She should've accepted Darrell's offer," he said.

Elizabeth shrugged. "I guess she was too much in love with your father to do that."

*****

After Eli served dessert and sat down at the table again, Elizabeth looked at Jonah.

"Your mother and I were never close," she said. "But I wish I'd taken the brief chance I had to warn her about your father."

Jonah and Eli stared at Elizabeth.

"Did you know," Eli asked, "Jonah's father was in love with you?"

"He came to see me," Elizabeth replied, still looking at Jonah, "the evening before he went to see your mother on his eighteenth birthday."

"He came to see you," Jonah asked, "the evening before the day he told my mother he wouldn't marry her?"

106

"Yes, the evening before that awful day. He told me Daniel would never disobey his mother and marry me. I'd have to find some other man to marry."

"He didn't know Daniel," Jonah said.

"No, he didn't," Elizabeth agreed. "But he'd decided he should take the place of Daniel in my life. I can't deny he was physically attractive enough, but I could never love him. Everybody knew he'd promised to marry your mother when he turned eighteen. He even admitted that to me. But then he was perfectly willing to abandon her as if she and you meant nothing to him. Maybe I should've told him how disgusting I thought he was. Maybe that would've convinced him he should forget about me and marry your mother. But I simply told him I could never stop loving Daniel, no matter what."

"Who could fault you for that?" Jonah asked. "You chose to tell him the truth without insulting him."

"But I wish I'd gone to see your mother that night when I still had the chance. I would've warned her. At least she would've known what to expect when your father showed up."

Jonah shook his head. "Maybe she would've met him with the shotgun at the door."

"Maybe. I deeply regretted what your mother did. On the other hand, I can't say I blame her. Pulling that first trigger must've given her a satisfaction the rest of us will never know."

*****

After Elizabeth, Eli and Jonah finished eating their supper, they took what was left of Eli's blackberry pie and vanilla ice cream out to the deputies. They offered to bring them water and whatever else they needed to make the long night hours pass as comfortably as possible.

When Jonah went out to check in with the deputies one last time before the Daleiden household went to bed, he saw Olivia slowly driving her black Buick along the road toward the house. She stopped her car when she reached the driveway.

"Excuse me," Jonah said to the deputies. "I'll take care of this."

"You know her?" one of the deputies asked.

"She's harmless," Jonah said, heading down the driveway

toward the road.

Olivia had the driver's window down. She laughed when Jonah approached her car.

"I guess Elizabeth's little gang isn't so brave after all," she said. "I see you've begged the sheriff to protect you, after that stunt you and Elizabeth's lawyer pulled in court today. What do you queers call that? Coming out of the closet? And you've got my grandson doing it, too. What fun you must've thought that would be. I'm not surprised Elizabeth goes along with it. I swear, that woman was born a witch. She'll do anything it takes just to be different and cause trouble."

Jonah didn't dare follow through on his desire to give Olivia a slap across her face. He'd no doubt go on to strangle her with his bare hands. Within sight of two sheriff's deputies, too.

"We didn't ask the sheriff to protect us," Jonah said. "Posting the deputies here was his idea. He didn't give us a choice."

Olivia laughed again. "You'll believe anything Elizabeth tells you. I'm sure she arranged it. Darrell Glendenning always did take her side. Why, he came into my house one day and told me I just had to let my Daniel marry that atheistic slut. I told Darrell hell would freeze over before I'd approve such a thing. Then I took back the cookie I'd offered him when he first came in with Daniel. I told him to leave. He was no longer welcome in my house."

Jonah chose to make no response to those disclosures.

"Darrell has a thing for women who murder men," Olivia said. "He told Daniel he offered to marry your mother when she was pregnant with you. And even after you were born. He must have some kind of death wish."

Jonah remained as stoic and silent as Violet in the courtroom.

"I actually hope Darrell succeeds in protecting all three of you," Olivia said. "I don't want you dead. Unlike my evil daughter-in-law, I don't have the mind of a murderess. No, I want to see your faces up there in that courthouse when the jurors announce their guilty verdicts. When you find out Elizabeth will spend the rest of her life in prison. When you face the fact she'll lose her precious farm here. When she gets the punishment she so richly deserves. When you and my grandson you've seduced finally see the truth and admit you're wrong."

Torture, Jonah had no doubt, could be so much more satisfying than murder.

Olivia laughed. "I can't wait to hear those words: 'Guilty.' 'Guilty.' 'Guilty.' I'm like a child looking forward to Christmas."

Guilty was the last word Jonah wanted to hear.

"Elizabeth is losing her case, Jonah. I'm sure even you can see that. But you and her pathetically incompetent lesbian lawyer are trying to make it into some kind of anti-queer thing. You know that has nothing to do with the crimes Elizabeth committed. You're just showing the world how desperate you are."

Olivia gave Jonah one last triumphant smirk and drove off.

*****

The next morning Elizabeth, Eli and Jonah sat in the back of a sheriff's car on their way to the courthouse in Oxford. Two deputies occupied the front seat.

Darrell Glendenning had promised them his deputies would bring them home when the trial was adjourned later that day. In fact, his deputies would accompany them to and from wherever they needed to go. They'd do so until he decided Elizabeth, Eli and Jonah could once again safely move about on their own.

"In other words," Eli said to Elizabeth and Jonah, "we'll be living under house arrest for as long as Sheriff Darrell Glendenning wishes."

Elizabeth shrugged. "If house arrest keeps us alive, I'm all in favor of it. Isn't that what the secret service does for presidents and their families? Would you call that house arrest?"

*****

The media on the courthouse steps had questions, though, as soon as Elizabeth, Eli and Jonah arrived and it became evident the Concord County sheriff had placed them under his protection.

But Darrell in his uniform was also on the courthouse steps ready to answer those questions.

"Why do the defendant, her son and Mr. Neumeyer need your protection?" Jill asked.

"My office has received calls," Darrell said. "So have the Daleidens. Some of the callers have threatened to kill them and Mr. Neumeyer."

Neither Jill nor any of the other reporters saw fit to challenge Darrell on that point.

"But my deputies and I," Darrell assured them, "won't let it happen."

Although Jonah hadn't known the current Concord County sheriff could've been his stepfather, his grandmother had told him some young men still came around after his mother was pregnant. A few did so even after she'd given birth to him.

One of them, from some political family in Oxford, had gone so far as to promise his mother he'd treat Jonah as if he were his own son.

Jonah looked up at Darrell in the late-summer sunshine on the courthouse steps that morning and smiled. He must've been the suitor his grandmother had described.

Chapter Seventeen

On Friday, August 5, Tanner called his fourth witness. Thane Sorenson was an attorney in the largest and most prestigious law firm in Oxford. His brother, a Taft, Goldwater and Reagan Republican who'd served as congressman from 1929 to 1959, still headed the firm. Jonah knew Thane had to be in his seventies.

"Your Honor," Tanner said, "the defendant's attorney and I have stipulated that Mr. Sorenson can testify as an expert witness on the probate- and property-law aspects of this case. We've provided Your Honor with the stipulation as well as Mr. Sorenson's curriculum vitae."

"I've read the stipulation, and I'm well aware of Mr. Sorenson's qualifications," Gideon said. "He may certainly testify as an expert witness in this case. It's a pleasure seeing you in my courtroom, Mr. Sorenson."

Thane took his eyes off Jonah and Eli for a moment and smiled at Gideon.

Tanner began his direct examination. "Are you familiar with the legal status and history of the real property the defendant, Elizabeth Daleiden, owns in Concord County, Illinois?"

"Yes, I am," Thane replied.

"Could you explain why you're familiar with the legal status and history of the defendant's real property?"

"Yes. You asked me to familiarize myself with her holdings so that I could testify as an expert witness in her trial. I agreed to do so."

"How did you do your job?"

"I reviewed all the pertinent public documents related to her property I could find. I also reviewed the documents you obtained as a result of a subpoena you served on a Chicago bank."

"Has either my office or the defendant paid or agreed to pay you for your services?"

"No."

"You've done your work pro bono, without pay or the promise of any pay?"

"Yes."

"What, if any, real property does Elizabeth Daleiden currently own?"

"She owns two adjoining quarter-sections in Revere Township two miles south of the village of Revere. She owns an east quarter-section and a west quarter-section. That's three hundred twenty acres altogether."

Jonah understood Thane's purpose as a witness was to establish that Elizabeth had motives to kill her father and neighbors.

And once again, Violet was letting the jury know Elizabeth had nothing to hide. She did have motives to commit all three of the murders she stood accused of. She had no need to contest those issues, as long as a knowledgeable expert witness Violet and Tanner could agree upon would tell the story.

Thane was the witness they'd chosen.

*****

"Did Elizabeth come into ownership of her two adjoining quarter-sections at the same time or at different times?" Tanner asked.

"At different times," Thane replied.

"Could you explain how Elizabeth became the owner of her east quarter-section?"

"It passed to her when her father, Jacob Reifert, died on May 25, 1950. He left no will. Elizabeth was his only heir under the Illinois intestacy law. Because she was an eighteen-year-old woman, she was legally of age. She hired an attorney here in Oxford to file a petition to have her father's estate administered in the probate court. When that proceeding concluded, she quitclaimed the east quarter-section to herself and Daniel Daleiden as joint owners of the property with the right of survivorship. I'm very sorry to say Mr. Daleiden died on December 26, 1976. So currently Elizabeth is the sole owner of the east quarter-section."

"Why do you say Elizabeth was her father's only heir under the Illinois intestacy law?"

"Intestacy means the dead person had no will. Elizabeth's father had no spouse when he died. The only woman he'd ever married, Elizabeth's mother, Emma, died in 1937, thirteen years before Jacob did. Elizabeth was Jacob Reifert's only child. Therefore, she was his only heir."

"Under Illinois law, was Jacob Reifert obliged to leave all of his property to his only child, Elizabeth?"

"No."

"Was he legally obliged to leave any of his property to Elizabeth?"

"No."

"Mr. Sorenson, can you explain your last two answers for the court and the jury?"

"Yes. Under the Illinois law in effect in 1950, as well as today, Jacob Reifert could've left any part of his property, or all of it, to anybody he pleased. He could've left it to another relative or relatives, a friend or friends, a charity or charities, or any combination of those. Under Illinois law then and now, all he had to do to disinherit his daughter was to sign a properly drafted and witnessed will."

"And in the will he could've left Elizabeth none of his property?"

"That's right. He didn't even have to explain why he wasn't leaving anything to her. All he had to do was to leave everything to another person or persons in his will. That would've left Elizabeth with nothing."

"And Jacob Reifert could've done that up to the moment he died?"

"That's right, Mr. Howland."

*****

"Turning to the west quarter-section, Mr. Sorenson, can you tell us when Elizabeth Daleiden became the owner of that property?"

"Yes. That occurred on December 17, 1955."

"What happened on December 17, 1955, that gave Elizabeth ownership of the west quarter-section?"

"The previous owners of the west quarter-section, Henry Hassenauer and Titus Peltz, died."

"Could you explain, Mr. Sorenson, why Elizabeth Daleiden became the owner of the west quarter-section upon the deaths of Mr. Hassenauer and Mr. Peltz?"

"When Henry Hassenauer and Titus Peltz bought the property, they owned it jointly with the right of survivorship. That meant if either of them died, the other would automatically become the sole owner of the property. Then, in 1945, Henry and Titus signed papers changing the ownership of the property. After that, there were three joint owners with the right of survivorship."

"Who were the three joint owners then?"

"Themselves and Elizabeth Reifert. That was, of course, the defendant Elizabeth Daleiden's maiden name."

"How old was Elizabeth when Henry and Titus made this change?"

"She was thirteen."

"That arrangement was still in effect in 1955, when Henry and Titus died?

"Yes, it was."

"And that's how Elizabeth became the owner of the west quarter-section?"

"Yes. It was by operation of law. No court proceedings were necessary. Soon after the deaths of Mr. Hassenauer and Mr. Peltz, she signed a properly prepared, notarized and recorded quitclaim deed making herself and her husband, Daniel Daleiden, joint owners of the property with the right of survivorship. As I testified before, Daniel Daleiden died on December 26, 1976. Elizabeth once again became the sole owner of the west quarter-section."

"Your Honor, I have no more questions for this witness. Thank you, Mr. Sorenson."

*****

"Ms. Sutherland," Gideon said, "you may cross-examine the witness."

"Mr. Sorenson, let's first consider Elizabeth's east quarter-section. How did Jacob Reifert, the defendant's father, come to own it? Did his family leave it to him? Did he buy it?"

Thane once again took his eyes off Jonah and Eli in the first row of spectators. He'd occupied a front-row seat himself during earlier sessions of Elizabeth's trial and her pretrial hearings. He turned to Violet at the defendant's counsel table.

"The answer is no to both of your questions," he replied. "The property belonged to Elizabeth's mother, Emma. Emma's uncle had left it to her in his will."

The spectators in the courtroom began murmuring, but not loud enough for Gideon to bring down his gavel.

"What was the uncle's name?"

"Karl Bachman."

"What was the name of Elizabeth's mother, before she married Jacob Reifert?"

"Her name was Emma Bachman."

"How did Jacob Reifert become the owner of the one-hundred-sixty-acre farm Karl Bachman left to his niece, Emma Bachman?"

"The same day Emma married Jacob, in 1931, she quitclaimed the property to herself and him as joint owners with the right of survivorship. If it matters, Emma was thirty-five years old that day, and Jacob had recently turned twenty-one. When Emma, Elizabeth's mother, died six years later, Jacob, as Emma's survivor under her wedding day deed, became the sole owner of the property."

The look on Tanner's face revealed he hadn't previously heard this part of the story. He couldn't object to the testimony of his own expert witness, though, without giving it even more attention than it had already gained in the courtroom.

Thane's testimony had proved Jacob Reifert possessed the legal right, based on the wedding day deed, to deprive Elizabeth of her mother Emma's farm.

Thane's testimony had also raised a question: What sort of human would do that?

*****

Violet wasn't done with Tanner's expert witness.

"Now, Mr. Sorenson, I'd like to call your attention to the west quarter-section Elizabeth Daleiden currently owns. Do you know when and how Henry Hassenauer and Titus Peltz became the owners of that property?"

"Yes, I do. They bought it in 1903. They paid cash for it. I found no mortgage documents recorded against the property during the time they owned it."

"How did they own the property?"

"Through a land trust. A Chicago bank was the trustee. Henry and Titus—and later, Elizabeth—were the beneficiaries of the trust."

"What's the purpose of owning property through a land trust?"

"The usual purpose is to conceal the identity of the owners."

"In the case of Henry and Titus, could their purpose have been to conceal the fact that they didn't share a last name and therefore weren't brothers, as they claimed to be?"

"If that was their purpose, a land trust would've been highly advisable."

"Who did Henry and Titus buy their property from?"

Thane looked at Elizabeth and took a deep breath.

"Henry and Titus bought their property from Karl Bachman."

"Was that person the same Karl Bachman who left the east quarter-section to Elizabeth's mother, Emma Bachman Reifert?"

"He was the same Karl Bachman."

Once again, Tanner—not unlike almost every other person in the courtroom that day—was unprepared for his own witness's testimony.

Violet continued. "When did Karl Bachman become the owner of the property he sold to Henry and Titus?"

"Two days prior to the day he sold it to Henry and Titus. He bought the property from his neighbors. He made nothing off the transactions, though. The amount Henry and Titus paid him was precisely the amount he paid his neighbors."

"Would such a purchase followed by a quick sale have helped conceal the fact that two men who weren't brothers were buying the property?"

"It would've accomplished that rather nicely. Together with the land trust."

"And Elizabeth's great-uncle, Karl Bachman, had to have been a knowing party to that transaction?"

"Without question."

"Did Karl Bachman ever marry?"

"No. His obituary in the *Oxford Times* described him as a 'lifelong bachelor.' His only survivor was Emma."

*****

116

After Tanner and Violet both said they had no further questions for Thane, Gideon adjourned the trial for the day—and, the day being Friday, for the week.

Before they left the courtroom to face the reporters and cameras on the courthouse steps, Violet introduced Tanner's expert witness to Elizabeth and Eli. She was aware that Thane and Jonah needed no introduction.

Elizabeth invited Thane to join her, Eli and Jonah at her house the following evening for drinks and supper. Violet and Belle would also be present.

Thane readily accepted Elizabeth's invitation. It wouldn't be the first meal he'd shared with Violet and Belle.

"Are you sure that's what you want to do, Thane?" Jonah asked. "The sheriff has deputies posted outside Elizabeth's house. I can only imagine they'll recognize you."

"You're asking me if I want to be seen in the company of you and Eli."

"I can understand why you might be hesitant to have that happen," Jonah said.

Thane laughed and looked at Eli.

"Please take your friend home now. I know you have chores to do. You may assure him when I arrive at your mother's house tomorrow, I'll go out of my way to compliment the deputies on the superb job they're doing protecting the two of you and Elizabeth."

"I'll take him home now, Mr. Sorenson," Eli said, "and tell him that."

Thane laughed again. "Please call me Thane, Eli. I'm certain you've noticed Jonah does."

Chapter Eighteen

A year previously Jonah had worked on a bank deal with a lawyer who was the founding partner of a LaSalle Street firm less than a tenth as large as Jonah's. Paul Sikorski in his seventies was as meticulous as Jonah was in his twenties. Leaving, as Paul said, "no stone unturned, no exception unconsidered," they worked late together several nights in Paul's office.

One evening during a supper they shared at the Berghoff, Jonah told Paul he grew up on a farm in Concord County.

Paul smiled when Jonah mentioned that.

"A lawyer who lives and works in Oxford is a friend of mine," he said. "His older brother was the congressman from that area for many years."

"You're talking about Congressman Eric Sorenson's brother?" Jonah asked. "Thane?"

"Yes," Paul replied. "Have you met him?"

Jonah shook his head.

"Thane and I," Paul said, "were in the same class at Northwestern Law School. That was in the Twenties. We thought times were changing. We planned to live together in Oxford after we graduated. Thane bought a beautiful old house in the wealthy part of town. He intended to work in his father's law firm. I'd try to start my own firm there."

"What happened?"

"Brother Eric brought those plans to an abrupt end. He told me I couldn't live with Thane. I was a gold digger son of a Chicago steelworker. I was taking advantage of Thane's misplaced affection. And it would be best if I didn't live or practice law in Oxford at all. Eric said he was planning to run for Congress. He didn't want people whispering about his family. If Thane didn't agree to my exclusion from his life, Eric would make it difficult for him, too, to live and work in Oxford. Thane certainly wouldn't work in his family's law firm."

Jonah decided to get to the point.

"I assume you and Thane planned to be more than roommates in Oxford."

Paul smiled again.

"Your assumption is correct. We would've been more than roommates."

"And Thane chose his family over you?"

"Thane chose his family. And I chose to move on. I came to Chicago and started my firm. I tried to find somebody to replace Thane in my life, but none of the men I met came close. Neither Thane nor I have ever had, with anybody else, what we know we could've had with each other. But we have kept in touch over the years. We are good friends at least."

Jonah and Paul successfully completed the deal they were working on. They understood what their clients would and wouldn't accept. They found mutually agreeable ways to accommodate them both.

When the holidays arrived that year, Paul invited Jonah to dinner at his apartment on Lake Shore Drive. The only other guest would be someone who'd expressed an interest in meeting the young lawyer who'd grown up on a farm in Concord County.

Paul's other guest that night was Thane Sorenson.

*****

"I have a question for you, Violet," Eli said, after taking his seat at his mother's dining room table Saturday evening.

"Let's hear it," Violet said.

Eli and Violet shared a love for volleyball. They played as a team against Elizabeth, Belle and Jonah, and the two-person squad almost always won.

"When you cross-examined Thane," Eli said, "you seemed to know exactly what he was going to say. Did you and he rehearse his testimony?"

Violet looked at Thane. They both laughed.

"No," Violet replied. "When Tanner and I agreed on Thane as an expert witness, we also agreed, in writing, not to speak with Thane about Elizabeth's case until he testified. So after that, Thane and I never spoke at all, other than to say hello in court or on the street."

"That's true," Thane said. "Violet and I couldn't speak about Elizabeth's case. So we chose not to speak at all."

Belle threw up her hands.

"What else was there to speak about?" she asked. "We suddenly had a person among us who might go to prison for the rest of her life for murders we knew she didn't commit."

Eli turned to Violet again.

"You've spoken about my mother's case with Jonah," he said.

"I had no agreement with Tanner not to speak with Jonah," Violet replied. "He was Tanner's witness before I got involved in the case. Jonah and I were free to speak about it as much as we pleased."

Jonah laughed. "And that we've done. But now, may I offer a possible answer to Eli's question?"

Belle laughed. "If it's only a possible answer, I can't see what harm it will do."

"Eli wants to know," Jonah said, "why Thane's testimony on cross-examination appeared to be rehearsed. Let's face it. It did appear rehearsed. The lawyer seemed to anticipate everything the witness said. Tanner must be tearing his hair out this very moment wondering—like you, Eli—how it happened. He was greatly surprised by the testimony of his own witness on cross-examination. So how did that happen? Allow me to speculate."

Belle laughed again. "Please speculate."

"Violet readily agreed with Tanner on Thane, the former congressman's brother, as an expert witness," Jonah said. "That's because she knew Thane was a careful and thorough lawyer. She also knew he'd look at the evidence from as many possible angles as he could. She wisely guessed he'd peer into the past and find what she and Elizabeth knew was there. And that's exactly what Violet wanted to come out. Elizabeth's east quarter-section belonged to her mother, Emma. Elizabeth's father took ownership of the property only through the wedding day deed and Emma's early death. And Elizabeth's great-uncle Karl was the person who made it possible for Henry and Titus to appear to be brothers when they bought the west quarter-section in 1903. Henry and Titus were connected with Elizabeth's family for more than five decades."

Violet nodded her head. "That's some good speculation, Jonah."

Thane, though, shook his head.

"I have to disagree, Jonah. You give me too much credit for being a careful and thorough lawyer. I was merely curious."

"Careful and thorough lawyers," Jonah rejoined, "are curious lawyers."

"I agree with that," Violet said.

Jonah looked at Eli and shrugged.

"There's always more to the story," he said.

*****

Jonah turned to Elizabeth. "Didn't Henry and Titus vote? Didn't they have licenses to drive? I seem to remember they had a car. Didn't they have bank accounts?"

"Henry and Titus voted," Elizabeth replied. "They had a car, licenses to drive it and bank accounts to keep their money in. They were normal hard working farmers."

"I was wondering about that myself," Thane said. "How did Henry and Titus do those things without revealing they had different last names?"

As she often did when she spoke of Henry and Titus, Elizabeth had tears in her eyes.

"I'll let you in on a secret," she said. "They had a forged birth certificate for Titus. They paid a forger in Chicago to do it for them. It burned up in the fire, but I saw it a number of times. Henry obtained a duplicate of his birth certificate from the clerk of the county where he was born. He claimed he'd lost the original. The forger cleanly erased Henry's first and middle names and the date of his birth. In a pawnshop she found the same kind of typewriter the clerk's office used to make Henry's duplicate. She borrowed it for half a dollar to type in Titus's first and middle names and the date of his birth. Nobody ever questioned the document. Karl advised Henry and Titus not to use it, though, when they bought their farm. That was too important, he told them, for a forged birth certificate, no matter how skilled the forger was."

"Well, good for Henry and Titus," Jonah said. "Their resort to crime didn't hurt anybody, and it achieved its purpose for them."

"And good for the forger," Belle said, "for doing her job so well nobody ever questioned what she did."

"Good for them all," Elizabeth said, "Uncle Karl included, for learning how to survive in this world."

"For getting away with it," Thane said, almost whispering.

Belle had described the look Thane gave Jonah and Eli in court as "wistful."

Chapter Nineteen

The next Monday morning, August 8, Tanner's fifth witness was Olivia Daleiden.

"Olivia knows absolutely nothing about the death of my father, or about the deaths of Henry and Titus," Elizabeth told Eli and Jonah on the way to the courthouse with Darrell Glendenning's deputies. "Whatever she says about them will be a lie."

When Tanner called her name, Olivia stood up from her seat in the first row of spectators, looked down at Eli and Jonah and smiled as if they might soon take her side. And, with proper apologies from them for ever believing Elizabeth, and promises they'd never speak openly again about their disgusting homosexual love for one another, she'd accept them as her allies.

After all, they were guilty of no worse offense than Daniel was—falling under the spell of that witch, Elizabeth.

*****

"How many children did you and Mr. Daleiden have?" Tanner asked.

"One," Olivia said. "Daniel. He's dead now. He was only forty-four years old when he died. His own wife, the defendant, prevailed upon his doctors to remove his life support. They were the doctors she hired. She had the money from her farm to pay them to do that. God knows, I attempted to stop them. I tried to save my son. But Elizabeth and the doctors removed Daniel's life support and let him die before I was able to obtain a court order forcing them to explain why they thought they could get away with murder. Daniel was already dead when the deputies delivered the order to the hospital. Elizabeth and the doctors ignored it."

Jonah knew Violet could've objected to everything Olivia said after the first word of her testimony. Olivia's other remarks added nothing to her answer to Tanner's question. But again, Violet and Elizabeth persisted in their strategy of letting all the witnesses, even Olivia, have their say in full.

"When was the last time you saw your son, Daniel, alive?" Tanner asked.

"Christmas Day last year, 1976. In his hospital room."

"Was Daniel's wife, the defendant, present in the hospital room the last time you saw your son alive?"

Olivia glared at Elizabeth.

"Yes, she was."

"Did you speak with her?"

"Yes. I told her if she went ahead with her plan and let the doctors remove Daniel's life support, she'd be murdering my son."

"What did she say?"

"She didn't say anything then. She simply picked up the room phone and asked for the hospital security people. They came right away, with their hands on their guns. They told me I had to leave. To them, it wasn't a matter of Elizabeth's killing Daniel. No, I was the guilty party. I was creating too much of a ruckus by simply opening my mouth to object to my son's murder."

"Did you leave the hospital?"

"I felt I had to. I was scared. That's the way Elizabeth does things. She uses brute force. She intimidates people. She makes them fear they could be her next victim."

Olivia's testimony was so objectionable it took Jonah's breath away.

Still, Violet said nothing. She merely exchanged glances with Elizabeth.

"After you left the hospital, did you have any occasion to speak to Elizabeth again last Christmas Day?"

"Yes, I did. I summoned the courage to go back to the hospital a second time."

"Were other people present then?"

"No, they'd all gone home. They'd seen Daniel alive for the last time. They had other things to do. It was Christmas Day. Even my grandson, Eli, had gone home to do the evening chores. The place he'd sat in all day on his father's bed was empty."

"Were any hospital personnel in the room?"

"No. They were in the hospital cafeteria enjoying an evening meal together. It was Christmas for them, too. They were singing carols. I could hear them from Daniel's room."

"Did you speak with Elizabeth?"

"Yes, I did. I told her I'd hired a lawyer. He was going to court in the morning to get an order signed by a judge. It would stop her and the hospital from killing Daniel."

"Did Elizabeth respond to that?"

"Yes. She shut the door to Daniel's room so only I could hear her. I think Daniel, no matter how much they had him sedated, could also hear what she said, but that didn't stop her."

"What did she say to you after she closed the door to Daniel's room?"

"The first thing she did was, she grabbed me by my neck with both her hands. She pushed me up against the wall. She's strong, you know. From all that farmwork she does. I was so frightened. I thought she meant to strangle me, right then and there. I'd be another of her many victims."

"We'll let Olivia tell her story," Violet told Eli, Belle and Jonah the Sunday afternoon before Olivia began her testimony, "no matter how outrageously false it might be."

They were at the picnic table in the shade of the oak trees on Elizabeth's lawn.

"We won't interrupt her," Violet said. "We won't be rude. We have no need to be."

"What did Elizabeth do then?" Tanner asked Olivia.

"She told me Daniel wouldn't be the first person she murdered. Then she laughed. She was only eighteen, she said, when she committed her first murder."

"Wow," Jonah heard Jill whisper to the reporters sitting next to her.

Wow for the entertainment of their viewers and readers, Jonah thought. Wow for the profitability of the companies they worked for.

And he suspected that same wow was what Violet and Elizabeth wanted.

"What did Elizabeth do then?" Tanner asked.

"She threw me down in a chair and stood over me—like some kind of monster in a nightmare. I was so frightened I just sat there listening to the awful things she told me."

"Did Elizabeth tell you," Tanner asked, looking at Elizabeth, "who she murdered when she was only eighteen years old?"

"She told me she murdered her father."

Gideon ignored the gasps from the spectators.

"Jacob Reifert?" Tanner asked.

"Jacob Reifert, her father."

"Did Elizabeth tell you how she murdered her father?"

"She came home one afternoon from school. She found her father in his bed, where she expected to find him at that time of the day. Everybody knew the poor man was an alcoholic. She took his pillow and covered his face with it. She pressed down on it and suffocated him. He woke up and struggled, but he couldn't get her off him. I told you she was strong. Her neighbors said she could do anything with a bale of hay their menfolk could do. Even when she was younger, none of the boys at school dared give *her* an unwanted feel. She'd take her foot and go straight for their you-know-what. She never did that to my Daniel, though. Of course, she never needed to. Unlike so many of those other boys, Daniel was a gentleman."

During the commotion that followed those remarks, Jonah turned to Jill.

"I hope you don't leave the defendant's foot out of your story this evening."

"For you and Eli," Jill said, "I'll try to keep it in."

After Gideon's gavel restored order, Tanner resumed questioning Olivia.

"Did Elizabeth tell you when she murdered her father?"

"She did, but she didn't have to tell me. I knew when it happened. It was at the end of May in 1950. Elizabeth and Daniel had only a few days left before they'd graduate from high school. What Colby Smith said was true. It was the same day something else happened in Revere Township. Elizabeth bragged to me how clever she was for choosing to murder her father that day. She knew the authorities were busy with all the reporters who'd come out from Chicago for the other business. She knew it was so shocking nobody would pay any attention to the unremarkable death of an alcoholic in his own bed."

Olivia looked at Jonah.

"What was the other business that day?" Tanner asked.

"An eighteen-year-old girl killed the father of her one-year-old boy with a double-barreled shotgun. She did it after he told her he wouldn't marry her. They were both eighteen. They'd been in the same class in school with Daniel and Elizabeth. When the sheriff's deputies came to arrest her, she at least had the decency to use the second shot to kill herself."

Gideon had to use his gavel again.

As soon as silence returned to his courtroom, Olivia resumed her testimony, without waiting for Tanner to ask her another question.

"The son of that young woman who shot his father and then killed herself is present in this courtroom today. He previously testified. Now he's sitting next to my grandson in the first row of spectators. There they are, behind Elizabeth. They live in the same house with her. They have no shame. They tell the world they're homosexual lovers. But of course that makes no difference to Elizabeth Reifert Daleiden, the defendant in this case. If murder is okay, why isn't what her son and his boyfriend are doing okay? Why isn't anything anybody wants to do okay?"

*****

"During your conversation with Elizabeth last Christmas Day, did she say anything to you about the sheriff's deputies who responded to her call concerning her father's death?"

"She most certainly did. She laughed and called them incompetent. One of the deputies—that was Colby Smith—could see Elizabeth's father had put up a tremendous struggle before he died. There was a broken lamp on the floor. He was entangled in his sheets."

Tanner again seemed to Jonah strangely unprepared for his own witness's testimony.

"But Sheriff Glendenning," Olivia continued, "didn't want to hear what Colby had to say. He had reporters in his office asking him about the other eighteen-year-old girl who'd killed her boyfriend with a shotgun. Elizabeth knew what she was doing when she picked that day to kill her father. If the authorities thought Jacob Reifert had been murdered, Elizabeth would have to be the one who did it."

"Elizabeth told you that?"

"She bragged about it. She said she was the only person on the face of the earth, other than her father himself, who had access to their house. She was the only person in the world who could've murdered her father in his own bed. And more than twenty-six years later, Elizabeth was still mighty pleased with herself. I sat in that chair in Daniel's hospital room and prayed to God she didn't have a pillow for me. When the nurses found me, she'd undoubtedly convince them I'd had a sudden heart attack or a stroke. After all, I was extremely upset about the execution she'd scheduled for my son the very next day."

*****

"Did Elizabeth explain to you why she killed her father?"

"She did, but as I said before, it wasn't necessary for her to tell me. She was eighteen and claimed to be in love with my son Daniel. That's why she killed her father. And Daniel dared to tell me he was also in love with her. She'd twisted his mind around so much he was willing to say something that horrific to his own mother."

"Elizabeth killed her father because she was in love with Daniel?"

"Yes. Her father had threatened to go to a lawyer and have a will written. He'd make certain Elizabeth wouldn't inherit his farm. He'd leave it to his nephews and nieces. Even though he'd never laid eyes on any of them."

Gideon held up his hand to indicate to Tanner he'd ask the next question.

"Do you know why Jacob Reifert made that threat?"

"I do. Elizabeth talked Daniel into getting married after they finished high school. But Jacob opposed their marriage just as much as Daniel's father and I did. Being eighteen, Elizabeth could marry without her father's consent. But Daniel couldn't marry without his parents' consent until he was twenty-one. And my husband and I refused to give our consent. That was when Elizabeth persuaded Daniel to live with her without the benefit of marriage. And that was when Jacob told Elizabeth if they did that, he'd write her out of his will."

Gideon wasn't done. "Would you tell us why you, Daniel's father and Elizabeth's father opposed the marriage of Elizabeth and Daniel?"

"Daniel's father and I raised our son to be a good Roman Catholic. Elizabeth Reifert wasn't even a Protestant. She had no religion at all. Going to church on a Sunday morning was something other people did, but not her. Her father at least went to a Lutheran church when he was growing up. He didn't want his daughter to marry a Roman Catholic any more than Daniel's father and I wanted our son to marry a woman who wasn't a Catholic. Both Elizabeth and Daniel knew their parents vehemently opposed their marriage, but they persisted in their foolish teenage romance anyway. They enjoyed their defiance. Not even God himself could stop them."

"I see," Gideon said, glancing at Tanner. "You may resume questioning your witness."

Olivia didn't wait for a question.

"And let's face it. Elizabeth did get away with murder After her father was dead, she no longer had to fear he'd sign a will leaving the farm to his nephews and nieces. As soon as he died, the farm was legally hers, as Thane Sorenson said. She knew it would be. Even at eighteen, she knew that. She's not a stupid person. Far from it. She knows how to use the law to her advantage. She knows how to use people to her advantage."

Olivia let her eyes rest on Eli and Jonah.

"So Elizabeth came right out and told you last Christmas Day," Tanner asked, "she murdered her father to get the farm?"

"Yes. And after she got it, she could do with it whatever she pleased. And that included moving Daniel into the house with her within a week. They weren't married, but that didn't matter to them. They lived in sin in that house for three years. They could've waited until they were twenty-one and married before they lived together. But nobody could talk reason to those two. I asked a priest to go out there to see Daniel and persuade him to repent his sin. But as soon as the priest arrived, Elizabeth ordered him off her property. She even threatened to call the sheriff and have him charged with trespass. Imagine charging a priest with trespass simply because he wished to save a parishioner's soul."

Chapter Twenty

Jonah was too young to remember anything about the three years Elizabeth and Daniel lived unmarried in her recently deceased father's house. But he could recall when they got married. He was four years old. His usually dour grandmother spoke of the occasion as if, at long last, something good had happened in the world.

Jonah could also remember a supper table conversation he had with his grandmother when he was ten years old. That rainy spring afternoon, while he was at school, she'd gone to see Elizabeth, Daniel and their new baby boy.

"What a cute little guy he is," Jonah's grandmother said. "Unfortunately, Daniel's mother arrived shortly after I did. And as soon as she showed up, she got into a loud argument with Elizabeth and Daniel. She said two people who'd lived in sin for three years could never be fit parents. She told them she had an appointment to see a lawyer in Oxford. She planned to get a court order declaring Elizabeth and Daniel unfit parents and placing the baby boy in the care of her and Daniel's father. She said they'd raise him to be a proper Roman Catholic who attended church every Sunday."

Ten-year-old Jonah wrinkled his nose at the thought of that. The few times his grandmother had taken him to the Congregational church in Revere he hadn't enjoyed himself. During what was called the "sermon," he invariably fell asleep. He was grateful, though, his grandmother, unlike the parents and grandparents of other dozing children, made no attempt to wake him until the sermon was over and it was time for another song.

Jonah's grandmother continued her story with a sigh.

"When I said I thought Elizabeth and Daniel would be perfect parents, Daniel's mother asked me why she was supposed to believe I knew anything about proper parenting. Daniel told his mother he didn't care for that insult at all, and she'd have to leave. Elizabeth told her she could either walk out on her own, or they'd call the sheriff to put her out."

Even then, Jonah understood Olivia based her slur on what his mother had done.

"And that Olivia," Jonah's grandmother said, "never once asked to hold her grandson. All during my visit, I held him on my lap. And despite Olivia's loud and angry threats, that little boy never raised a peep."

Jonah's grandmother went to work on her pork chop and buttered baked potato with her fork and knife and shook her head.

"I wanted to wrap my fingers around Olivia's scrawny neck and strangle her right then."

Suddenly, though, Jonah's grandmother, perhaps in the grip of schadenfreude, smiled.

"Elizabeth and Daniel have named their boy Eli," she said. "After her."

*****

"Was the murder of Elizabeth's father," Tanner asked, "the only murder Elizabeth admitted to you last Christmas Day?"

"Heavens, no," Olivia replied. "She told me she'd committed two other murders. She also bragged about not getting caught for those. She was smug, I must say. I'm still grateful to God I got out of that hospital room alive. My son Daniel wasn't so fortunate. Elizabeth has committed four murders that I know of, including Daniel's. And yet, even now, I see people in this courtroom sobbing—wasting their tears only because Elizabeth might finally have to pay the price for what she's done in her miserable life."

During that last remark, Olivia had her eyes fixed on Eli, Jonah and Belle.

Violet had placed Tanner in a difficult position. If she made no objection to the relevance of Olivia's testimony, how could he? She was his star witness in the case he hoped would take him to Congress, maybe even the governor's office or the United States Senate.

"I want to focus now," he said to Olivia, "on the two other murders Elizabeth admitted to you when you spoke with her last Christmas Day. Did she name those two victims?"

"Yes, she did. They were her neighbors, those two elderly men, Henry and Titus. We used to think they were brothers and had the same last name, Hassenauer. It turned out they weren't brothers at all. The younger one had a different last name. It was Peltz."

"Elizabeth admitted to you that she killed Henry Hassenauer and Titus Peltz?"

"Yes, she did."

"Did Elizabeth tell you when she murdered them?"

"Once again, she didn't have to tell me when she did it. It was the night their house burned down. It was a terribly cold Saturday night in December. It must've been 1955. I was there. So was Elizabeth. Even Mr. Neumeyer tells us he was there, when he was six years old. He's probably telling the truth about that. He would've been there, with his grandmother. They were neighbors. They lived only a mile or so down the road from them. His grandmother was like Elizabeth, you know. She did outdoor work on her farm and told people she enjoyed it."

"Did Elizabeth tell you how she murdered Henry Hassenauer and Titus Peltz?"

"She fed them rat poison. She put it in their supper that Saturday evening. She watched them die, sitting in the chairs where the deputies found them. After she was certain they were dead, she set their house on fire."

"Is that what Elizabeth told you last Christmas Day?"

"Yes, that's what she told me. But Daniel knew nothing about those murders. I got her to admit to me Daniel was innocent all along. He knew nothing about any of her murders until she admitted them to me in his hospital room. I'm sure he could hear her, but what could he do then? My son was an innocent boy living with a murderess so coldhearted she could freeze hell itself."

Once again, Olivia chose to spend more than a few moments looking at Eli and Jonah, as if they might be two more innocent boys living with a murderess.

"Elizabeth told you she put rat poison in the food she fed Henry and Titus for their supper on Saturday, December 17, 1955?"

"Yes, she told me that. She'd told Daniel she was fixing their suppers. She didn't tell him anything about the rat poison."

"And then Elizabeth told you she watched Henry and Titus die?"

"She also told me that."

"And Elizabeth also told you she set their house on fire after she was certain Henry Hassenauer and Titus Peltz were dead?"

"She told me she set their house on fire. Then she went home and pretended to be surprised when Daniel saw the flames."

"Did Elizabeth tell you why she set the house on fire after she

135

killed the two old men?"

"She did. She was quite proud of herself for starting that fire. She wanted to make it look as if the neighbors murdered the old men and set their house on fire."

"Why would the neighbors want to murder the old men?"

"Because they were homosexuals. For years, those men had lived on that farm posing as brothers. Then it turned out, shortly before they died, they weren't brothers. They'd lied when they said the younger one, Titus, had the same last name as Henry. The story went around that Henry and Titus were men who enjoyed other men the way God wants men to enjoy women, and only women. I heard what the people at the fire were saying. Mr. Neumeyer was telling the truth about that, too. Many of those people claimed they were glad to see the two men dead—they got what was coming to them. And Elizabeth used that to her advantage. The sheriff had to tell the reporters exactly what Elizabeth wanted him to tell them."

"And what was that?"

"That the old men died as a result of an accident. In their old age, she told the sheriff's deputies, the men slept in chairs in front of their fireplace. They liked to build roaring fires in it that sometimes sent burning embers out onto the wooden floor. Titus would get up with his boots on and stomp out the flames with no harm to himself or Henry. This time, apparently, he wasn't fast enough. So his and Henry's deaths were accidental. Nobody murdered them."

Jonah remembered he'd told Olivia this story when she came to see him in Chicago.

"Sheriff Royal Glendenning bought Elizabeth's story," Olivia continued, "to quell rumors that a mob had murdered Henry and Titus. You should've heard her tell me about it. She was so pleased with herself for putting it over on the sheriff. 'The people kept electing that man,' she told me, in her sassy, know-it-all way, 'and I kept using him.'"

Once again, Tanner couldn't help himself. He glanced at the allegedly duped sheriff's grandson, Warren Glendenning, in the first row of spectators and seemed close to laughing.

Maybe they wouldn't oppose one another on the ballot in the next primary election. Maybe, after Tanner won three convictions of murder against Concord County's most notorious serial killer ever,

Warren would realize he couldn't stay in the race for Congress without risking a loss by such a large margin it would keep him from running for any elected position again.

*****

"Did Elizabeth explain to you why she murdered Henry Hassenauer and Titus Peltz on December 17, 1955?"

"She confirmed what I'd always suspected."

"And what was that?"

"She was impatient. She was tired of taking care of them. She had a strange relationship with those men. Everybody knew that. They signed some papers with a lawyer in Chicago that meant they'd leave their farm to her, a neighbor girl who wasn't a relative, when they died. They obviously didn't know her the way I did. As soon as people found out those men weren't brothers but something quite different, she saw her chance to kill them off and claim immediate ownership of the farm they'd been stupid enough to leave to her. Some rat poison in their supper on a cold winter night was all it took for her to do it. She knew she'd never need their house. She gladly set it on fire. That's just what a mob would do, she told me. They'd murder the old men and set their house on fire with them still in it to cover up what they did."

Olivia looked at Elizabeth and laughed.

"She also admitted to me she suffered a terrible scare that night. The volunteer firemen put out the fire before it completely burned the kitchen, and she'd left the empty rat poison container on top of whatever else was in the kitchen garbage pail. It didn't burn up. And one of the deputies saw it there and gave it to Clyde Lewis. But Elizabeth later found out the old Sheriff Glendenning, Royal, destroyed it. So she got away with her second and third murders in five years."

Olivia had her eyes fixed on Elizabeth.

"But how many more victims," she asked, "has Elizabeth murdered in the twenty-two years since? One at least that I know of—my son, Daniel."

*****

Tanner concluded his direct examination of Olivia late in the afternoon. Violet's cross-examination would have to wait until Tuesday.

At the supper table Monday night, Eli begged Jonah to give him and his mother his truthful opinion as a lawyer.

"Based upon what the jurors have heard so far," he asked, "can they find Mom guilty of three murders?"

"I won't lie to you," Jonah said. "They can. Violet predicted this would be a difficult case to win. She was right."

"The jurors can find Mom guilty," Eli asked, "beyond a reasonable doubt?"

"Yes. Tanner has provided more than sufficient evidence that your mother had the motive, means and opportunity to commit each of the three murders. And now he's presented evidence that your mother admitted committing them."

Eli shook his head. "If the jurors want to believe my crazy grandmother."

"If they want to believe her," Jonah said.

Elizabeth looked at Eli and shrugged.

"I'm sorry," she said, "but Violet would agree with Jonah, word for word. At this point, I can only testify and hope they believe me and not Olivia."

Chapter Twenty-One

On Tuesday, August 9, Violet remained seated next to Elizabeth at the defendant's counsel table when she began her cross-examination of Olivia.

"Olivia, did you visit your son Daniel during his last stay in the hospital here in Oxford?"

"Of course I visited Daniel. He was the only child his father and I ever had."

"During your visits, were you aware that Daniel was in pain?"

"I knew that, yes. I was his mother."

"Did Daniel tell you he was in pain?"

"Yes, he did. That's the sort of thing boys tell their mothers."

"Did Daniel tell you he was in so much pain he wished to die? Did he tell you he wished to have his life support removed? Did he tell you he just wanted to die and be done with the pain?"

"No. Daniel would never say such things. He was a good Roman Catholic boy. He didn't believe in suicide."

"But Daniel did believe a good Roman Catholic man was free to marry a woman who wasn't a Catholic, even a woman who had no religion at all?"

"That was Daniel's one and only flaw. Elizabeth knows how to seduce men into doing her bidding."

Olivia chose to glance at Eli and Jonah again.

"Do you remember visiting Daniel about three weeks before he died when your grandson Eli was present and when Daniel could still speak with his visitors?"

"Eli was sometimes present when I went to see Daniel."

"When Daniel could still speak, was he coherent?"

"Yes. With me, he was."

"Could you understand what he said?"

"Of course I could. I was his mother."

"Do you remember Daniel asking Eli to pull out all the plugs on his life support machines? Do you remember a nurse who was present telling Eli to not even think about doing such a thing because it would be murder?"

Olivia glared at Eli.

Jonah realized what Violet was doing. Olivia could guess Violet had Eli and the nurse prepared to testify about the incident. The jury might think Eli would lie to keep his mother out of prison—but would the nurse?

"That might've happened," Olivia said.

"It did happen, did it not?"

"It did happen."

"So why did you lie in this court and say Daniel never said, in your presence, he wanted his life support removed?"

"I didn't lie. I misspoke."

"You didn't lie? You merely misspoke? You'll say whatever you please, true or not, to make sure your daughter-in-law Elizabeth is convicted of murder, won't you?"

Tanner, as if recovering from a sucker punch, rose from his chair.

"Your Honor, I must object," he said.

"I withdraw the question," Violet said.

*****

"Olivia, you testified that Elizabeth admitted to you in Daniel's hospital room last Christmas Day she committed three murders?"

"Yes, that was my testimony."

"When did you report those admissions to State's Attorney Tanner Howland?"

"I did that in April."

"Why did you wait so long?"

"I didn't think anybody would believe me. Then Jonah Neumeyer paid Elizabeth a visit and got her to admit to him no mob killed Henry and Titus and set their house on fire. When I heard that, I realized Elizabeth had blundered badly."

From her seat on the witness stand, Olivia looked down at Elizabeth and shook her head.

"How had Elizabeth blundered?" Violet asked.

"She told Jonah the truth. No intruders, no mob killed those two old men and set their house on fire. She hadn't told him the whole truth, but she didn't need to. It was obvious. Elizabeth could only know intruders or a mob didn't do those things if she did them herself. That's when I went to see Mr. Howland."

"You made a statement to State's Attorney Tanner Howland, didn't you?"

"Yes, I did."

Violet looked down at her papers on the table and picked up a stack of them stapled together in the upper left corner. She held the document in front of her.

Tanner stared at it as if it had arrived magically from another world.

"Mr. Howland had a court reporter present taking down every word you said, didn't he?"

"Yes, a court reporter was present. Tanner told me that's what she was doing."

"Olivia, you testified in this court yesterday that Elizabeth admitted to you she killed her neighbors, Henry and Titus, by putting rat poison in their supper?"

"Yes, that's what Elizabeth told me."

Violet turned to a page in the document and appeared to be reading it silently.

"But when you made your statement to Tanner, you didn't say anything about rat poison, did you?"

Olivia stared at the document as intently as Tanner did.

After a long pause, Gideon turned to Olivia.

"Please answer the last question," he said.

"It's possible," Olivia said, "I didn't say anything about rat poison to Mr. Howland."

"Yes or no, Mrs. Daleiden," Violet said. "Did you say anything about rat poison to Mr. Howland?"

"No," Olivia replied.

"When Mr. Howland asked you how Elizabeth killed Henry and Titus, didn't you tell him you didn't know how she did it?"

"It's possible I said that."

"Yes or no, Mrs. Daleiden."

"Yes, I said that."

"Didn't you also tell him you were too afraid to ask Elizabeth how she did it?"

"Yes, that's what I said."

"But didn't you testify yesterday in this court that Elizabeth

141

bragged to you how easy it was to kill Henry and Titus with rat poison?"

"Yes, I said that yesterday?"

"Why did you lie?"

"I didn't lie. I merely added what Clyde Lewis made evident last week. Whoever murdered the two old men did it with rat poison. Since it was Elizabeth who murdered them, she must've done it with rat poison."

"But Elizabeth never told you that, did she?"

"No, she didn't."

"She never admitted anything to you about murdering anybody, did she? You made up her so-called admissions in Daniel's hospital room from beginning to end, didn't you?"

Tanner once again rose from his chair.

"I withdraw the questions," Violet said.

*****

"You also testified in this court yesterday about another admission Elizabeth supposedly made to you last Christmas Day. Didn't you testify that Elizabeth admitted the bedroom where her father was found dead was in disarray, due to the struggle he put up to keep her from suffocating him with his own pillow?"

"Yes."

"Would you please speak up so the jurors can hear you?"

Olivia reluctantly turned to the jury.

"I said yes."

"But that isn't what you said in your statement to Mr. Howland, was it?"

"No."

"In fact, you told Mr. Howland that Elizabeth was proud of herself for killing her father so efficiently he looked as if he died peacefully—as if his liver finally gave out and he passed away quietly in his sleep. Isn't that what you told Mr. Howland?"

"Yes."

Olivia wasn't enjoying her cross-examination by Violet nearly as much as she had her direct examination by Tanner.

"Why did you change your story when you testified in this

courtroom?" Violet asked.

"I didn't change my story. Colby Smith testified Jacob Reifert's bedroom was in disarray, as if Jacob had put up a ferocious struggle to stay alive. I merely updated my testimony to make it consistent with what Mr. Smith said."

"You call changing what Elizabeth told you a mere update in your testimony?"

"That's how I see it."

"You don't see it as proof of your lie?"

"What lie?"

"Your lie that Elizabeth admitted to you last Christmas Day she killed her father. And didn't you do the same thing with your other lie?"

"What other lie?"

"Your lie that Elizabeth admitted to you she killed Henry Hassenauer and Titus Peltz. You already told us you changed that lie in order to accommodate the rat poison testimony of Clyde Lewis."

"I'm not lying. I'm only trying to do what God wants me to do. I know in my heart Elizabeth murdered her father and her homosexual neighbors to get their farms."

"And you think that gives you the right to come into Judge Gideon Heidecker's courtroom and lie repeatedly about a conversation with Elizabeth you never had?"

Once again, Tanner rose to his feet.

"I withdraw the question," Violet said. "I'm certain the jury can figure out the answer to it without any input from this witness."

"Wow," Jill whispered in Eli's and Jonah's ears.

"Wow," Jonah whispered back.

*****

After Elizabeth, Eli and Jonah finished their chores that evening, the deputies drove them to Oxford. Belle was once again in charge of supper.

"You've got to explain this," Eli said to Violet, who was sitting next to him at the table. "And I'm not going to let you and Jonah get away with any of your legal bullshit this time."

Belle laughed. "We certainly don't want any legal bullshit in this house. Although Dickens got away with it more than once. I think it depends upon the story, Eli."

"What am I supposed to explain?" Violet asked Eli, taking his hand in hers as if that might help placate him.

"Oh, come on," Eli said. "How did you get a copy of the statement Olivia made to Tanner? It was obvious they didn't know you had it before you began your cross-examination."

"That's a damned good question," Jonah said, turning to Violet. "How on earth did you get it?"

"I found it on the floor one morning when I stepped into my office."

"Who put it there?" Eli asked.

Violet shrugged her shoulders.

"Let me guess," Jonah said. "Somebody in the state's attorney's office worked late the previous evening, waited until everybody else was gone, put on a new pair of gloves, made a copy of the statement at the Xerox machine, hand-delivered the fingerprint-free copy to your office, and slipped it under your door."

Violet laughed. "I can only assume something like that happened."

"And Tanner found it out," Jonah said, "as soon as you started talking about Olivia's statement. He realized somebody in his office had gotten a copy of it to you. Somebody who knew the value of a prior statement when you confront a liar."

"I can see that," Belle said. "Liars tend to confuse their stories. They don't have the anchor of the truth to cling to."

"Let me make another guess," Jonah said, still looking at Violet. "You found the copy of Olivia's statement just before you filed your motion for an early trial."

"Another good guess," Violet said. "Elizabeth and I had already figured out what Colby Smith and Clyde Lewis would say on the witness stand. We knew for sure what you and Thane would say. Then, all of a sudden, we knew what Olivia would say."

"And you wanted the trial to begin as soon as possible," Jonah said. "Before Tanner found out he had a traitor in his office who gave you a copy of Olivia's statement."

"Right again, Jonah," Violet said. "Are you a lawyer just

pretending to be a farmhand?"

"I have a question," Elizabeth said. "Was that traitor in the state's attorney's office secretly working for Warren Glendenning?"

"No doubt," Violet replied.

Jonah laughed. "Warren seemed as pleased with your cross-examination of Olivia as I was."

"But isn't it possible," Belle asked, "that person in Tanner Howland's office was secretly working to make sure an innocent person wasn't sent to prison for the rest of her life?"

"That's the version of the story I prefer," Jonah said.

Violet looked at Eli and sighed.

"They'll always be dreamers," she said.

Elizabeth looked across the table at Violet and Eli and raised her glass of wine.

"You've both chosen well," she said.

Chapter Twenty-Two

Tanner decided to ignore the questions Violet had raised about the honesty of his star witness. On Wednesday, August 10, he informed Gideon he had no further questions for Olivia and would call no additional witnesses. He rested his case.

And once again, Violet chose not to follow tradition and move for a directed verdict for the defendant. She'd promised the media numerous times Elizabeth would testify. A motion for a directed verdict at the close of the state's attorney's case, on the other hand, could lead the jury to believe Elizabeth didn't want to testify—might even be afraid to testify.

Violet also knew Gideon shouldn't grant such a motion even if he wanted to. She agreed with Jonah. Tanner had presented enough evidence, despite Olivia's dubious changes in her story, for the jury to find Elizabeth guilty of all three murders beyond a reasonable doubt.

"I want the jury to decide my case," Elizabeth had said at the supper table in Violet and Belle's apartment above the bookstore the previous evening. "If the jury wishes to send an innocent person to prison for the rest of her life, my hopes for this world were for naught from the beginning. I might as well find that out now."

Jonah nodded his head. "We might as well all find that out now."

Eli shook his head. "I don't know how you two can be so accepting of such a world."

Elizabeth looked at Eli without concealing her sorrow.

"What other choice do we have?" she asked. "I'm on trial. I have the right to tell the truth. I don't have the right to be believed. That's the way it should be."

*****

Violet called Elizabeth as her first witness.

As she'd done throughout the trial, except for the initial stipulations, Violet remained seated at the defendant's counsel table when she questioned Elizabeth.

"Elizabeth, did you hear Thane Sorenson testify that your mother's uncle, Karl Bachman, wrote a will leaving your mother, Emma Bachman, his one-hundred-sixty-acre farm, which is now the east half of your farm?"

"Yes," Elizabeth said.

"How, exactly, were Emma and Karl related?"

"Emma's mother, Anna, my grandmother, was Karl's sister."

"Where was your mother Emma living when she inherited her uncle Karl's farm?"

"She was living with Karl on his farm."

Tanner rose from his chair.

"Your Honor, I object to this line of questioning. How far back in time do we need to go? We've already heard testimony that the defendant inherited the east half of her farm from her father because he died, or was murdered, before he had a chance to write a will. What do the defendant's mother and great-uncle have to do with the three murders in 1950 and 1955 that the grand jury charged the defendant with committing?"

Gideon spoke before Violet had a chance to.

"Mr. Howland, you exercised no control over your witnesses. You let them say whatever they wished, no matter how much hearsay, conjecture and apparently irrelevant information they had for us. The defendant's counsel could've objected to, or asked me to instruct the jury to ignore, at least ninety percent of the testimony of your last witness. Ms. Sutherland graciously chose not to. Now I'm afraid you have no choice but to listen to what the defendant has to say in her response to all of that. I'll let the defendant and her attorney provide as much background in this case as they reasonably feel they need."

Tanner sighed and sat down.

"Don't forget, Mr. Howland," Gideon continued, "you have the right to cross-examine the defendant. I'm sure the spectators sitting in the second and third rows of the courtroom are especially looking forward to that. Meanwhile, your objection is overruled. Ms. Sutherland, you may continue questioning your witness."

"Could you explain," Violet asked, "how your mother came to live with her uncle Karl?"

Elizabeth turned to the jury. "My grandmother Anna lived in Chicago. Her only income was the money men gave her to have sex with them. Then one of her customers murdered her."

Gideon had to use his gavel, more than once this time, to quiet the spectators.

148

"How old was your mother," Violet asked, "when that happened?"

"She was nine."

"What year was it?"

"It was 1905. My mother was born in 1896. When Anna got killed, Emma had nobody in the world but Karl to turn to. A judge in Chicago appointed him Emma's legal guardian. He brought her back to his farm in Revere."

"Was that when your mother met Henry and Titus?"

Tanner rose to his feet again. "Your Honor, the defendant's mother isn't on trial."

"Objection overruled," Gideon said, turning to Elizabeth. "You may answer."

"Yes," Elizabeth replied. "Henry and Titus lived next door. They and Karl exchanged help, as neighboring farmers did in those days. But the three of them never seemed to need or want any other neighbor's help."

Elizabeth, knowing she could get away with it, turned to the reporters in the gallery.

"The man who murdered my grandmother, Anna Bachman, was eventually electrocuted," she said. "The story was on the front pages of all the papers. Henry and Titus and I went to the public library in Chicago one winter day and looked them up. My grandmother was the victim in that story—the person the reporters called 'Anna, the fallen woman in apartment E.' They never gave her last name. Due to her profession, I suppose. Nobody here in Concord County knew she was Karl's sister and Emma's mother. Nobody but Karl, Henry, Titus and Emma. They knew. It was one more dark secret they shared."

*****

"How long," Violet asked, "were Henry Hassenauer and Titus Peltz your neighbors?"

"For the first twenty-three years of my life. From the day I was born in 1932 to the day they died in 1955."

"During the time you and they were neighbors, did you know they weren't brothers?"

"During the last ten years of that time, yes, I knew they weren't brothers."

"How did you come to know that?"

"They told me."

"Do you remember how old you were when they told you?"

"Yes, I do. I was thirteen."

"Did you feel free to tell other persons Henry and Titus weren't brothers?"

"No."

"Why not?"

"Henry and Titus asked me not to tell their secret to anybody else."

"Did you know why they wanted other people to think they were brothers?"

"Yes."

"How did you know that?"

"They told me."

"And what reason did they give you?"

"They were what we'd now call gay. They didn't want other people to know."

"And they told you that when you were thirteen years old?"

"Yes."

"Elizabeth, where were you living when you were thirteen years old?"

Only five people in the courtroom, or the world, knew the answer to that question: Elizabeth, Eli, Violet, Jonah and Belle.

"I was living with Henry and Titus," Elizabeth replied.

*****

"How old were you, Elizabeth, when you began living with Henry and Titus?"

"I was five years old," Elizabeth replied.

"Oh, God," Jill murmured, giving a whispered voice to the expressions on the faces of the jurors and almost all the spectators.

"What year was it," Violet asked, "when you began living with Henry and Titus?"

"It was 1937, the year my mother died."

"How old were Henry and Titus then?" Violet asked.

"Henry was born in 1870. He was sixty-seven. Titus was born ten years later, in 1880. He was fifty-seven."

As the judge, jurors and spectators visibly struggled with the information that a five-year-old girl lived with two men that old, Elizabeth smiled.

"We're in a different world here," Jill whispered.

"They were both still physically fit then," Elizabeth said. "To a surprising degree. They did the work much younger men did. I saw them do it."

*****

At the supper table that evening, Jonah had a question for Elizabeth.

"Who was your mother Emma's father?" he asked.

Elizabeth smiled. "Anna told my mother she didn't know for sure who her father was. Anna had an attractive young client during the time in question. She hoped Emma was his child. She'd let him have sex with her without using any protection. The one time my mother saw him was when Anna pointed him out to her in a German-speaking crowd on Lincoln Avenue. My mother also began hoping he was her father and would someday marry Anna and live with them. The poor deluded girl. His family owned a construction company that built high-rises in the Loop. He'd gone to college. He never would've married a lady of the night."

"That man was your grandfather?" Eli asked. "My great-grandfather?"

"Apparently so."

"How well did Emma know Karl," Jonah asked, "before she came to live with him?"

"Quite well, actually. When he was a young man, Karl often took the train to Chicago on Saturday nights. He'd be all cleaned up, desperately attempting not to look like a farmer but fooling nobody. Anna told Emma his inability to pass as a city boy no doubt accounted for his popularity among the men like himself he went in search of in

Chicago. He sometimes met them in strange places like public parks at night. But he'd always first stop to visit his sister Anna and his niece Emma. Sometimes he'd only see Emma because Anna was alone with a client all the time he was there. On those occasions, he'd often take Emma to a restaurant for supper."

Eli turned to Jonah. "Do gay guys still meet up in the parks in Chicago?"

"Frank tells me they do," Jonah replied.

*****

Jonah had another question for Elizabeth.

"How did Karl meet Henry and Titus?"

Elizabeth smiled again. "Somebody in Chicago who'd taken a liking to young farmers introduced them. Henry and Titus grew up on tenant farms near Bloomington. After Titus finished high school, they packed all their belongings in one suitcase each, said good-by to their families and took the train to Chicago. They found jobs in a factory. Their farm boy backgrounds didn't seem to stand in their way. They lived in a one-bedroom basement apartment. They got hot water when their landlord's family upstairs needed it for taking baths."

Jonah shook his head. "I'm sure that sort of life isn't what they wanted."

"No, it wasn't," Elizabeth agreed. "They had a goal. It required that they save their money. Henry already had some savings. For the last fourteen of his twenty-eight years he'd hired himself out to neighbors who appreciated strong, uncomplaining farmhands and paid a premium for their work."

"What was their goal?" Eli asked.

"They wanted to buy a farm of their own someplace where nobody knew them and they could pass themselves off as bachelor brothers. Then they'd be happy. They had no doubt they could save enough to buy a farm. What they enjoyed most in their lives, the company of the other, didn't cost them anything."

"How did they end up in Revere?" Jonah asked.

"Their best friend Karl learned his neighbors wished to sell their farm. The money Henry and Titus had saved by then fell short of the purchase price, so Karl loaned them the difference. They paid him off after their fourth year on their farm. They hadn't considered going to a bank and asking for a mortgage loan. Single men without stable family members available to cosign their notes weren't considered creditworthy."

"Was Karl in love with Henry and Titus?" Eli asked.

Jonah had wondered that himself.

"He certainly must've loved them on some level," Elizabeth replied. "They told me he looked out for them, especially during their first years on their farm. Karl made certain they got their crops in, even if it meant waiting to harvest his own and taking a risk he wouldn't get them in on time. If you're asking me whether he was intimate with them, I truly don't know. Henry and Titus never told me they were. I assume that means they weren't. But who can say for sure? In any event, it would've made no difference to me."

*****

Elizabeth, Eli and Jonah watched Jill's report on the ten o'clock news that evening.

"The triple-murder trial of Elizabeth Daleiden," Jill said, "continues to proceed in a highly unusual manner. Judge Gideon Heidecker allows the witnesses, including the defendant today, to simply tell their stories as they wish, with minimal adherence to the rules of evidence."

Jill played up the 1905 murder of the defendant's maternal grandmother in Chicago.

"We have confirmed that the murder was a sensational story at the time. Elizabeth's grandmother, Anna Bachman, was assumed to be the victim of a man who'd brutally murdered a number of women thought to be prostitutes. The killer was only convicted of Anna's murder because there was a witness to that crime. The killer didn't know it, but Anna's daughter Emma, Elizabeth's mother, was hiding in a closet. For her, the experience must've been especially horrific. When she witnessed Anna's murder, identified her killer and testified at his trial, Emma was only nine years old."

"God," Jonah said, as if he were religious.

Chapter Twenty-Three

The next morning, Thursday, August 11, Violet continued her direct examination of Elizabeth.

"Your mother, Emma Bachman, was thirty-five when she married your father, Jacob Reifert, in 1931?"

Tanner rose from his chair shaking his head.

"I'm sorry, Your Honor, but I don't understand why the defendant's counsel thinks the jury needs to know what happened in 1931. This case is about what happened on May 25, 1950, and December 17, 1955, which are the dates when the three victims in this case died."

"I agree with you," Gideon said. "But I'm quite certain I'll never know what happened, nor will you or the jury, unless we hear a full account of what led up to those dates."

With those remarks, Gideon, Violet and Elizabeth gained an unexpected ally from the first row of spectators.

"I agree," Olivia said. "Please, Tanner, let Elizabeth say whatever she wishes to say. We can all tell the difference between a truthful person like myself and a liar like her."

Neither Violet nor Tanner chose to object to those gratuitous comments.

And Gideon neither struck them from the record nor even acknowledged he heard them.

"Wow," Jill whispered again.

"Wow," Jonah whispered back again.

Gideon looked at Elizabeth. "You may answer the question."

"Yes," Elizabeth replied, "my mother was thirty-five at the time of her marriage to my father in 1931. When she was sixteen, in 1912, Karl's bull attacked and almost killed him. For the next eighteen years, my mother cared for him and did the work on his farm. Henry and Titus helped her, of course. My mother apparently never considered marriage, or pursued any romantic interests, until Karl died in 1930."

"And on the day of their marriage," Violet asked, "Jacob, your father, was twenty-one?"

"Yes. That's how old he was. As soon as some elderly neighbors took him into their house as their hired man, from God knows where, Emma put a claim on his attention. By then, my mother had inherited Karl's farm. She and Henry and Titus had long since given up on dairy farming. They raised hogs instead. They could inexpensively ship them to the stockyards in Chicago on a truck and get a fair price for them. They made some kind of profit almost every year, even in the Depression. They weren't the type of people who bragged about how well off they were. But the bank employees knew where they stood. So did the trucker, the farm implement dealer, and the family who owned the hardware store. And those people told others."

Elizabeth paused and turned to Tanner as if she wished to be certain he didn't object to her telling this part of her story.

The look on his face indicated he wasn't pleased with her testimony, but he remained seated and silent nevertheless.

"Many single men from miles around would've married my mother," Elizabeth continued. "But while she was caring for Karl and doing the farmwork, she never seemed to notice them. Then Karl died, and my father showed up. Henry and Titus couldn't fault her for finding him physically attractive. And she forgave him his preference for sulking rather than smiling. He claimed his parents, who were tenant farmers, were mean and unloving, and his seven older siblings had picked on him. She believed what he told her and felt sorry for him."

Elizabeth paused again. She'd noticed, as Jonah had, the ballpoint pen the juror in the middle of the front row was using had apparently gone dry. When the juror indicated she'd retrieved a fresh pen from her purse, Elizabeth resumed her testimony.

"Before my father would agree to marry my mother, he went to see a lawyer in Oxford. After that, he told my mother he'd marry her only if she signed a deed making him a joint owner of her farm and giving him the right of survivorship if she died before he did. The deed made no mention of the rights of any children they might have. Henry and Titus pointed this out to my mother, but she refused to listen to them. She was quite certain, she said, Jacob was her last chance for a husband. If she didn't marry him, she'd become what she called an 'old maid.' She told Henry and Titus they shouldn't be so suspicious of an innocent youth."

Elizabeth somehow smiled at the jurors even as she wiped away a tear.

"Henry laughed at that. What kind of innocent youth, he asked my mother, goes to see a lawyer before he agrees to marry a woman

156

he's supposed to be in love with? My mother insisted she could see nothing wrong with putting her new husband on the deed to her farm. They planned to run it together. If she died before he did, she was certain he would leave it to their children. Henry and Titus remained unconvinced. They nevertheless continued helping my mother and father with their work, especially in the last month or so before I was born."

*****

"How soon after your parents married," Violet asked Elizabeth, "were you born?"

"Nine months and a few days."

"And your parents, Emma and Jacob, had no other children?"

"I was their only child. Soon after I was born, my mother agreed with Henry and Titus she'd made a serious mistake. My father could never love anyone as much as he loved alcohol. He sometimes drank himself into a belligerent state. He'd start yelling, and I'd start crying. One night, when my mother couldn't get me to stop, he hit her."

"Where did he hit your mother?" Violet asked.

"In her face."

"Did he slap her?"

"No, he hit her with his fist, his closed fist. But she hit him back in his face with both her fists. And she hit him so hard he fell to the floor. She took advantage of him being so drunk. She jumped on top of him and held him down with her knees on his shoulders and her hands around his throat. She made no attempt, though, to punish him any further. She simply told him if he ever hit her again, she'd handle the matter another way."

"What," Violet asked, as if she and Elizabeth were speaking privately, keeping no secrets, "was the other way your mother said she would handle the matter?"

"She promised my father she wouldn't just knock him down. And she wouldn't need a weapon. She'd do it with her bare hands."

"What did your mother promise your father she'd do with her bare hands, Elizabeth?"

"She'd kill him."

*****

Gideon called what he referred to as a "brief recess" and left the bench. He undoubtedly knew any attempt by him to stop the jurors, reporters and other spectators from openly discussing Elizabeth's last remark would fail.

"It's called jury nullification," Jonah heard Jill say to her colleagues. "Even if Elizabeth clearly murdered her father, the jurors can still find her not guilty. Nobody can punish them for their verdict no matter how wrong it might be. And the state can't appeal an acquittal."

Jonah turned and looked at Jill.

"But how will the jurors find out they can do that?" Jonah asked. "You know as well as I do, Violet can't tell them."

Eli also turned and looked at Jill. Once again, he had tears in his eyes.

"Whatever you lawyers say about it," he said, "my mother never murdered anybody."

Gideon let the people in his courtroom speak of those and other possibilities until they brought themselves to order on their own and fell silent. Then he returned to the bench.

"You may continue questioning Elizabeth," he said to Violet.

*****

"Despite what happened," Violet asked, "did your parents continue to live together in your mother's house."

"Yes, they did," Elizabeth replied.

"Why did they choose to do that?"

The question was highly objectionable. Violet was asking her own witness to speculate on the reasons for what two other people, now deceased, had chosen to do forty-five years ago.

But Tanner had learned any attempt by him to thwart Elizabeth's testimony would draw glares from the jurors and snickers from his opponents among the spectators. And Gideon would simply rule, once again, Violet's question dealt with background. Tanner remained silent.

"After my mother threatened to kill my father," Elizabeth said, "he behaved himself. Henry and Titus could see he was afraid of her. And she told them she saw no reason to throw him out of her house and go to the bother of a divorce. As for my father, he got what he wanted. My mother let him drink. She gave him the money he spent at the bar in Revere. By the time I turned five years old, my mother, Henry and Titus did almost all the work on both farms. I remember seeing them do it. My mother took me with her, even out to the fields riding on her lap behind the horses. My father was either up at the bar or in the house, drinking. Maybe, as my mother believed, he had no choice in the matter. But I couldn't understand that then. I was afraid of him. I wouldn't go near him unless I was with my mother. I despised him."

"Did you previously testify that your mother Emma died when you were five years old?"

"Yes, that's how old I was when she died. Despite her mistakes, I loved her."

"How did your mother die?"

"She let my father drive her car. The three of us were on our way to Revere, she to buy groceries and he booze. She didn't realize he'd already begun drinking that day. She was on the passenger side of the front seat, pleading with him to slow down. I was on the floor between the seats with my fingers in my ears. That's where I always ended up when they yelled at one another in the car. Then my inebriated father topped off his refusal to slow down by attempting to pass a truck going up the hill south of Revere. My mother's screams were the last thing I heard before the collision."

Elizabeth paused, looked at Eli and suffered the guilt of a parent making her child cry.

"My father was lucky. At the last moment, he swerved to the left. He suffered some superficial cuts and bruises. I wasn't hurt at all, except for the loss of my mother. People always said she and the two persons in the other car died instantly, upon impact, without any suffering. I wasn't sure how anybody could know that, but I hoped it was true."

*****

"What happened to you," Violet asked Elizabeth, "after your

mother died?"

Tanner had no objection even to that open-ended, answer-any-way-you-please question.

"Henry and Titus came to get me at the hospital the day of the accident. They took me to their house. They had three bedrooms on their second floor. They'd never used two of them except for storage. I felt safe with them. They sat with me most of the first night. I couldn't stop crying. I knew my mother had died in the accident. 'She's dead,' I heard the truck driver say. 'She's dead,' I heard a sheriff's deputy say. 'She's dead,' I heard people in the crowd say. But no matter how much I pleaded with them, they wouldn't let me see her."

Elizabeth paused, revealing a dreadful silence in the courtroom. Apparently surprised by its intensity, she quickly resumed.

"Henry and Titus arranged for my mother's burial a few days later. My father showed up for it. He'd remained sober since the accident. He told Henry and Titus I'd have to go home with him. Otherwise, he'd call the sheriff and have them charged with abducting his child. Why did they worry anyway? He was off booze forever, he said."

"Did Henry and Titus give you back to your father?"

"Reluctantly. And after a lot of screaming on my part. They knew they didn't have a legal leg to stand on. Jacob was my sole parent then. Only he had the right to my custody. But I feared him more than I ever had before that. Far more."

"Why was that?" Violet asked.

"I no longer had the protection of my mother."

"Did your father remain sober?"

"No. He resumed drinking the next afternoon. When suppertime came, I asked him if he wanted me to help him prepare the meal. I'd tried to help my mother whenever I could. She liked to ask me to do things she knew a five-year-old-child could do. My father, though, said he wasn't hungry. He might not be hungry all night. He wasn't fixing supper for me no matter what. If I starved to death, why should he care? He never wanted to be a father anyway. He'd let that damned Emma talk him into it. And now he had a screaming five-year-old girl to take care of. Maybe, if I starved to death, I'd no longer be around to remind him of Emma."

160

Gideon closed his eyes and slowly shook his head. When he peered at the jurors again, he was in tears, as were most of them and many of the spectators.

"Did your father feed you anything that evening?" Violet asked.

"No. I went into the kitchen and made myself a peanut butter and jelly sandwich. The jelly was actually my mother's blackberry jam. Titus had taught her how to make it. I was sitting at the table eating it with a glass of milk when my father came into the room. He demanded to know who told me I could make myself a sandwich and help myself to the milk. He picked up the plate my sandwich was on and my glass of milk. He threw them to the floor, shattering them on the linoleum. 'Now you can clean up that mess,' he said. I screamed instead. He hit me."

Gideon laid his notebook down.

"Where did he hit you?" Violet asked.

"In my face."

"Did he slap you?"

"No, he hit me with his fist."

"A closed fist?"

"Yes, a closed fist."

"Did you suffer any cuts or bruises?"

"My cheek was bleeding. The left side of my face was black-and-blue and swollen for at least two weeks after that."

Gideon wept. His shoulders shook involuntarily.

"Your Honor," Violet asked, "should I pause?"

"No," he replied, wiping his face with his handkerchief. "I'm sorry. Please forgive me. Proceed with your examination."

Chapter Twenty-Four

"After your father struck you with his fist," Violet asked Elizabeth, "what did you do?"

"I picked up the biggest piece of the plate from the floor, threw it at him and ran as fast as I could."

"Where did you run to?"

"To the only place I knew I'd be safe, the house where Henry and Titus lived. I ran down the path between their orchard and garden. We still use it now to get to their barn and chicken coop. They called it Karl's path."

"What did your father do?"

"He was bleeding himself by then. He'd deflected the jagged piece of plate with the back of his right hand, the same hand he'd used to hit me. The china must've severed a vein. His injury was much bloodier than mine."

"Thank God for that," Jill whispered.

Without turning to look at her, Jonah could tell Jill also had tears in her eyes.

"He ran after me. But he had to run with his left hand around his right wrist to stop the bleeding. He was also drunk, of course. He stumbled and fell several times."

Elizabeth paused, catching her breath.

"When Henry and Titus heard me screaming and saw me running down the path with my face bleeding, they burst out of their house like two angry hornets. Titus brought along what he called his 'hunting rifle.' He never hunted anything with that gun, but he'd taught himself how to use it shooting at targets. Henry liked to let people know Titus was gifted with unusually keen eyesight. Henry said he could put a bullet in the middle of the forehead of a person hundreds of feet away. It was true, too. My mother had taken me to Titus's shooting range down by their creek to see for myself."

"Did your father catch up to you?"

"No. Henry yelled to Titus to give him a warning shot. I could see Titus pull the trigger. I thrilled when I heard the crack of the bullet. Titus shouted to my father the next one would find its mark—between his eyes. That's when my father gave up his senseless pursuit of a daughter he'd rather see dead anyway. Henry came to me, got down on his knees and took me in his arms. 'You're safe with us now,' he said.

'I'll never leave you alone with that man again.' Henry stood up and told my father he and Titus were taking me to the Neumeyers—Jonah's grandparents—so they could see what he'd done to me. And if he wanted to complain about my living with the two men who were my nearest neighbors, they'd simply ask the authorities to speak with the Neumeyers and hear what they had to say."

*****

"How long did you live with Henry and Titus," Violet asked.

"For the next thirteen years of my life, from 1937, when my mother died, to 1950, when my father died. After his death, Daniel and I moved into what Henry and Titus called 'Karl and Emma's house.' It's the same house I live in now with Eli and Jonah."

"Did anybody other than yourself, Henry, Titus and your father know you were living with the two much older men who were your neighbors?"

"Only Jonah Neumeyer's grandparents. Henry and Titus went to extraordinary lengths to conceal from everybody else the fact that I lived with them. When I was six and started school, one of them went with me to my father's house to meet the school bus every morning. And one of them was always waiting when I came home in the afternoon."

"Did the bus driver or your neighbors wonder why they did that?"

"Everybody except the Neumeyers thought Henry and Titus did it as a favor to my father. He was what people called a 'hopeless drunk' who'd caused a terrible accident that killed three people. They didn't know I lived with my elderly neighbors. They didn't know Henry and Titus packed my lunch for school each day until I learned how to do it myself. They didn't know I ate all my other meals with Henry and Titus. They didn't know I had two neighbors in place of my mother to protect me from my father."

"Why did Henry and Titus insist upon such secrecy?"

"They didn't want trouble. A child was supposed to live with her father. She wasn't supposed to live with the two men who were her nearest neighbors. Single men who weren't brothers weren't supposed to live together either. Henry and Titus had learned to be secretive about a lot of things."

"Did your father make any further objection to your living with Henry and Titus?"

"Heavens no. They did his work for him. They told me they were doing it for me. They considered the farm mine because it had belonged to my mother and my great-uncle Karl. They planted and brought in the crops. They fed, looked after and sold the livestock. They kept what they made off the farm in a special bank account in Henry's name. They even took care of my father. They supplied him with firewood. They bought him food and booze on their shopping trips to Revere."

Jonah noticed the juror in the middle of the first row was nodding her head, as if what Elizabeth said made sense to her.

"I eventually helped them do all those chores. Henry and Titus and I agreed keeping my father away from us—buying him off, maybe you'd have to call it—was worth the work. We liked working together anyway. We always laughed a lot. It made the work go faster. When people saw us doing fieldwork together, they thought we were simply neighbors exchanging help."

Elizabeth turned to the jury and smiled.

"Our contribution to the thrashing ring," she said, "was two old men and a teenage girl. But I never heard anybody complain about it. They couldn't say we didn't do our share of the work. We took our wagon to the thrasher more often than anybody else did. And there were other groups of three persons to a wagon. They were usually a farmer with two sons. Jonah Neumeyer's grandparents and mother, though, were another odd group like ours. But not even they could keep up with Henry and Titus and me."

Eli gave Jonah a consolatory hug.

"They made it into a game," Jill whispered. "You and your parents against me and my two gay friends. Sounds like fun."

*****

Going down the courthouse steps that afternoon, Elizabeth stopped when she, Eli, Jonah and the deputies reached Jill. Violet and Belle had chosen to remain behind.

"I understand," Elizabeth said, "you have a question for me."

"Did you murder your father?" Jill asked. "Did you kill him for what he did to you?"

"I'm sorry," Elizabeth replied. "Violet tells me I can't answer those questions yet. Not until I testify in court. I can't even give my son the answers to those questions, and I know it's driving him crazy."

"I hope you also know," Eli said to his mother, "I won't blame you at all if you did kill that man. And if I were on the jury, I'd acquit you anyway."

Elizabeth took Eli in her arms and hugged him before she turned to face Jill again.

"I can tell you," Elizabeth said, "I'm not a victim in this story."

"Is it important to you," Jill asked, "that, unlike your grandmother and mother perhaps, you not be seen as a victim in this story?"

"It's only important to me," Elizabeth replied, "that I tell the truth in this story."

*****

Jill interviewed a prominent criminal defense lawyer in his Loop office that evening. He explained what jury nullification was for her viewers. He described it as "a wonderful power American jurors possess."

As he spoke, Jill feigned increasing surprise.

"You mean to tell us," she asked, "even if the jurors fully believe Elizabeth Daleiden murdered her father, they can acquit her?"

"That's right," the lawyer replied.

"Even if they believe her guilty beyond a reasonable doubt?"

"Yes, even then."

"Will the judge or somebody else—I presume Elizabeth's attorney—tell the jurors they can do this?"

"It's most unlikely, Jill. The law doesn't allow them to do that. If Elizabeth Daleiden's attorney even mentions it, the judge will have to declare a mistrial and probably find her in contempt of court. I understand Violet Sutherland has represented defendants in criminal cases before. I'm sure she knows she can't say anything in the presence of the jurors about jury nullification."

"Wait a minute," Jill said. "The jurors in Elizabeth Daleiden's case possess what you call a wonderful power to acquit her even if they believe she's guilty. And nobody can punish them for doing it. But they won't ever be told they have this wonderful power?"

"That's right, Jill. Nobody will ever tell them they can't be punished in any manner whatsoever for finding Elizabeth not guilty of murdering her father, even if they're absolutely certain she did it. Nor could the state's attorney out there in Concord County appeal their not guilty verdict to a higher court. He'd be stuck with it. I'm sure he knows that, too."

Other reporters interviewed other criminal defense attorneys and law professors that evening, all of them talking about jury nullification.

*****

At Elizabeth's dining room table that same night, Belle had a question for Elizabeth.

"Where did Henry and Titus buy your clothes and other personal belongings? I can't imagine they took you to a store in Revere or Oxford. Wouldn't at least some of the salespeople and other customers wonder why two older men were buying such things for their neighbor's little girl?"

"I hope you didn't have to take the train all the way to Chicago," Jonah said.

Elizabeth looked at Belle and Jonah and smiled.

"Titus would spend hours with me leafing through the Sears catalogue. He often had a better idea of what I'd like than I did initially. I came to rely upon his judgment. He loved things for me that were rose, violet, pink, light blue, light green and pale yellow. Nothing bright red or orange would do for me, he said. No dark colors either. Not with my light-brown hair."

Belle laughed. "Titus wasn't just a hardworking farmer, a sharpshooter with his hunting rifle and a hot guy in bed for his big brother. He was also a young lady's fashion consultant."

"Whatever he and I decided upon," Elizabeth said, laughing herself despite her tears, "Henry wrote up the order and sent it off. He was certain nobody in the Sears catalogue office in Chicago would ever wonder or care why an old man named Henry Hassenauer in Revere, Illinois, was ordering clothes and other items for a little girl."

"The Sears catalogue," Belle said. "I should've guessed it."

"Me too," Jonah concurred.

"I don't blame Tanner Howland," Elizabeth said, "for thinking I murdered my father. I wouldn't fault anybody, not even the jurors, for coming to that conclusion. But Henry and Titus? I wanted them to live forever."

Chapter Twenty-Five

Proceedings began on Friday, August 12, with another request from Tanner for a private conference. Tanner, Gideon and Violet once again hovered over the court reporter, whispering. Tanner made part of his argument as he pointed toward the area where Jill, Eli and Jonah sat.

"I can't imagine what this is all about," Jill whispered.

After the sidebar concluded, Gideon announced his decision.

"Mr. Howland's motion for a mistrial is denied. Ms. Sutherland, you may continue."

*****

"Did you hear the testimony Olivia Daleiden gave in this case?" Violet asked.

"Yes," Elizabeth replied, her eyes fixed on her mother-in-law in the first row of spectators. "I hung on every word of it."

"Specifically, did you hear her testify that your father, Jacob Reifert, didn't want you to marry Daniel Daleiden?"

"Yes, I heard her say that."

"Was that true?"

"That part of her testimony was true."

"How do you know it was true?"

"After Daniel and I decided to marry as soon as we finished high school, I told my father what we planned to do. He told me he'd oppose our getting married any way he could."

"Did he tell you why he'd do that?"

"Yes. He told me I was the daughter of a Protestant, and Protestants didn't marry Roman Catholics. I asked him how long it had been since he'd attended a Protestant church. He told me that didn't matter. We were Protestants, and Protestants didn't marry Catholics. Besides, he said, Daniel Daleiden was, in his words, a 'pretty boy' who only wanted to marry me because he'd get a farm out of it. Otherwise, he'd never marry a woman who did a man's work on a farm. What was true for my father when he married my mother would be true for Daniel if he married me."

"Did you tell your father what you and Daniel would do if you couldn't marry?"

"Yes. I told him as soon as we graduated from high school, Daniel would move in with me. He and I would openly live together in Henry and Titus's house as if we were married. I'd no longer pretend I lived with my father."

"Was that in fact what you and Daniel planned to do?"

"Yes, it was. We knew if we had any children right away, they might be illegitimate for a while. But Henry took us to a lawyer who said we could make them legitimate as soon as we married, after Daniel turned twenty-one. So that's what we agreed to do. Henry and Titus were delighted. Daniel was fourteen when I suggested we pay him to help us do our fieldwork—even if he was a town boy we'd have to teach how to farm. By the time he and I were seniors in high school, he helped us with all our work. Henry, Titus and I paid him a share of our earnings from both farms. My father knew it, too. He didn't object to that part of the deal—the money part. But if Daniel and I lived together openly as if we were husband and wife, we'd be going too far. I don't think my father wanted me to be happy."

Violet looked down at her papers.

"I quote," she said, "from Olivia's testimony in this case: 'Her father had threatened to go to a lawyer and have a will written. He'd make certain Elizabeth wouldn't inherit his farm. He'd leave it to his nephews and nieces. Even though he'd never laid eyes on any of them.'"

Violet looked up from her papers.

"Did your father make that threat to you?"

"Yes, he did."

"But he didn't get a chance to carry out that threat, did he?"

"No, he didn't."

"Isn't it true he didn't because he died? Because he died just before you and Daniel graduated from high school? Just before you and Daniel started living together?"

Jonah marveled. Violet had embarked upon what amounted to a cross-examination of her own witness, her own client.

"Yes," Elizabeth said. "Thane Sorenson explained it. I inherited the farm the moment my father died because he never made a will. That solved all our problems. Daniel and I moved into Karl and Emma's house. We lived there as unmarried lovers until Daniel turned twenty-one, in 1953. My father's death made all that possible."

"Are you saying you had a good reason, on May 25, 1950, to want your father dead?"

"No, I'm not saying that. My years of happiness with Daniel, and later Eli, on our farm were worth a lot to me—but not worth another person's death, not even my father's death. I believed that then, and I still believe it now."

*****

"Did you hear Colby Smith's testimony about what happened on May 25, 1950, the day your father died?"

"Yes."

"I quote a question Mr. Howland put to Mr. Smith in this case: 'Do you know why you and the other deputy were sent to Jacob Reifert's farm in Revere Township on May 25, 1950?' Now I quote Mr. Smith's answer: 'As I understood it, his daughter, the defendant, had called the sheriff's office. She said she'd come home from school that afternoon and found her father in his bed. She claimed she couldn't wake him up, he wasn't breathing, and he had no pulse.'"

Violet looked up from her papers.

"Did you do and say that?"

"Yes, I did."

"Did you tell the sheriff's office the truth? You came home from school that day and found your father dead?"

"Yes, that was the truth."

"Did you look in on your father when you came home from school every day?"

"No. I almost never did that."

"Why did you do it on May 25, 1950?"

"I did it because of what Henry and Titus told me when I got off the bus."

Elizabeth looked at Eli and saw his tears. She squared her shoulders and continued her testimony.

"They no longer met me when I got off the bus from school. I was eighteen years old. My father couldn't possibly hurt me then. But that day both Henry and Titus met me at the bus."

"What did they tell you?"

171

"These were the first words Henry spoke to me after the bus left and nobody else could hear him: 'Your father is dead, Elizabeth. Titus and I killed him.'"

*****

Gideon once again called for a recess and left the bench.

Jill tapped Eli on his shoulder.

"Did you know before today," she asked, "Henry and Titus murdered your grandfather?"

"No," Eli replied, turning to Jill, letting his tears fall. "But I'm glad to hear they did."

"Do you believe your mother is telling the truth?"

"I know she's telling the truth. She always tells the truth."

*****

After Gideon returned to the bench, the spectators, reporters and jurors fell silent without being asked to do so.

"You may resume your examination, Ms. Sutherland."

"Did you hear Olivia testify that you told her only you and your father had access to his house?"

"Yes."

"Was that the truth?"

"No. Olivia made that up. My father wanted Henry and Titus to have access to his house. That was so they could bring him his firewood, his food, his booze and everything else he needed, whenever it was convenient for them to do so. When I was in school. When he was in a bar somewhere drinking. When he was asleep in his bed."

"Did Henry and Titus tell you how they killed your father?"

"Titus said they went into his bedroom while he was sleeping. They used his own pillow to suffocate him. Mr. Smith was right about that. Titus said my father struggled, but not as much as they thought he would. When they were certain he was dead, they put his pillow back where they found it. They wanted him to look as if he'd died in his sleep."

"Did Henry and Titus tell you why they killed your father?"

"We'd talked about it a number of times after my father made his threat to see a lawyer and write a will. They called my father the 'accidental owner' of Karl and Emma's farm. After my mother died, Henry and Titus strongly believed it should've been my farm. To them, my father was a worthless, drunken interloper. They said we'd already wasted enough of our time taking care of him. And they'd certainly never let him give my farm away to relatives he'd never met. They told me Daniel and I had a far better right to the farm than my father did. We should live together but not with two old men. We should start our life together in Karl and Emma's house. That's where both my mother and great-uncle would've wanted us to live."

"Did you agree they were justified in killing your father?"

"No. And I told them, over and over, I didn't agree with them about that. If I had to live my life without owning my great-uncle and mother's farm, I could do it. I didn't believe people should kill other people just to ensure happier lives for themselves."

Elizabeth paused and once again confronted a silence too unbearable not to break.

"I never thought," she continued, "Henry and Titus would actually murder my father. After they told me they did it, I said they'd made a serious mistake. They merely shrugged their shoulders. 'What's done,' Titus said, 'is done. This is your farm now. As it should be.' 'You and Daniel,' Henry said, 'can live together in your own house now.'"

*****

"Did Henry and Titus tell you why they chose May 25, 1950, to kill your father?"

"Mr. Smith was right about that, too. It was the day Jonah Neumeyer's mother killed his father and herself with a shotgun. The sheriff and his people were already dealing with hundreds of requests for information from the newspapers and radio and television stations concerning that business. We heard about it at school. Henry and Titus said nobody would pay much attention to the death of a hopeless drunk in his own bed. They proved to be right. The violent murder and suicide of two eighteen-year-old lovers were much more newsworthy."

173

*****

"What did you do after Henry and Titus told you they killed your father?"

"I went to my father's bedroom. It's the room Eli and Jonah use for their bedroom now."

"Did Henry and Titus go with you?"

"No, they didn't. They went back to their house."

"What did you find in your father's bedroom?"

"I found my father in his bed as Henry and Titus said I would. He wasn't breathing. He had no pulse. He was even turning cold. I went down to the phone in the kitchen and called the sheriff's office. I don't blame Colby Smith for thinking he saw signs of a struggle. But my father's whole house looked the way his bedroom did. When he was drunk, he knocked things over and left them where they fell on the floor, broken. After I no longer feared my father, I offered to clean up his house for him. He wouldn't let me do it, though. He said I'd remind him too much of my mother. I couldn't tell whether he was expressing contempt for her or regret that she was no longer around, still in love with him."

Gideon indicated to Violet he'd ask the next question.

"You were familiar with your father's house before he died?"

"I was often in his house delivering the things he needed. He let me fix a broken window once in the dead of winter when he feared his pipes would freeze. I saw how awful things were. I'm certain nobody in this courtroom would wish to live the way he did, even if it came with ownership of a one-hundred-sixty-acre farm and four people who did all the work for him."

Gideon continued his examination from the bench.

"Did you see any signs of a struggle in your father's bedroom?"

"No, I didn't. The broken lamp had lain on the floor so long the pieces were covered with dust. Mr. Smith didn't notice that. My father never slept peacefully. His sheets and blankets always ended up entangled. I argued with Mr. Smith that day simply because I knew the truth and he didn't. Henry and Titus said my father gave up his struggle far more quickly than they thought he would. Maybe by then he didn't care much whether he lived or died."

"Why didn't you inform the sheriff's deputies that Henry and Titus killed your father?"

"I didn't feel I had any duty to inform on Henry and Titus. Violet tells me I was right about that."

Elizabeth looked at Eli, once again with tears in her eyes.

"I never told anybody Henry and Titus murdered my father," she said. "I never told my husband Daniel. I never told our son Eli. I never told anybody until I found myself charged with murdering my father myself. Then I told my lawyer, Violet."

"You didn't think Henry and Titus should be brought to justice for killing your father?"

"To the kind of justice that would've sent them to death row and the electric chair? Could you imagine I might risk that happening to Henry and Titus? They'd raised me from the age of five and loved me as if I were their daughter. And I loved those two men as if they were my fathers."

Gideon remained silent after those remarks.

Elizabeth, though, continued her story.

"Daniel and I started cleaning and repairing Karl and Emma's house as soon as the deputies left with my father's body. We began living in it together the night we graduated from high school a few days later. For us, that was our wedding night. Henry and I came to see a lawyer here in Oxford. As Mr. Sorenson testified, the lawyer handled the probate court proceeding for my father's estate. When that was finished, I signed a deed making Daniel a joint owner of Karl and Emma's farm. I joyfully used the gift Henry and Titus gave me when they murdered my father. I wasn't about to tell the sheriff or anybody else what they did."

Chapter Twenty-Six

Darrell's deputies drove Elizabeth, Eli and Jonah to Thane's house in Oxford for supper Friday evening. Thane's other guests were Violet, Belle and Paul Sikorski. Paul had attended court that day.

During the appetizers and wine in Thane's living room, Jonah had an announcement for Violet, Elizabeth, Belle and Eli.

"We know Violet can't say a word to us about the private conference she had with Tanner and Gideon this morning. Thane and Paul and I have therefore decided to present our version of what they might've said. Thane has agreed to play the Honorable Gideon Heidecker. Paul says he'll be delighted to attempt to portray the brilliant defense attorney Violet Sutherland. And I, of course, can only stand in for the nasty state's attorney Tanner Howland."

Belle laughed. "The play's the thing—as long as you speak your words trippingly on the tongue."

Thane joined in the laughter. "I don't know if we'll rise to a Shakespearean level, but we can certainly give it try."

"I'll begin," Jonah said, looking at Thane. "Your Honor, I move for a mistrial. You must be as outraged as I am."

"What are your grounds for a mistrial, Mr. Howland?" Thane asked. "Why should I be outraged?"

"Every Chicago television station last night had a defense attorney or a law professor explaining jury nullification. I've never seen any-thing like it in my life. And it's obvious who was behind it."

"Your Honor," Paul said, "neither the defendant nor I had anything to do with what the Chicago television stations chose to show their viewers last night."

"Mr. Howland," Thane asked, "are you accusing the defendant or Ms. Sutherland of somehow instigating those jury nullification interviews?"

"Well, maybe not directly," Jonah conceded.

"Your Honor," Paul began.

"Indirectly, Mr. Howland?" Thane asked. "Do you have proof of that?"

"Isn't it obvious, Your Honor?" Jonah asked, turning to point his finger at Eli. "Look at them, the defendant's son and his lawyer friend sitting together in the first row. And those Chicago television reporters who did those jury nullification interviews last night are sitting right behind them. They've been whispering back and forth throughout this trial. And that one reporter, Jill Foster, she's a lawyer, too. She was in Mr. Neumeyer's class in law school."

"Your Honor," Paul said, "neither the defendant nor I have any responsibility for what her eighteen-year-old son Eli and his friend Mr. Neumeyer and those reporters sitting behind them say to one another. I don't know, and don't care to know, whether the subject of jury nullification came up among them or not."

"Look at them, Your Honor," Jonah persisted, still pointing at Eli. "They're smirking. They're laughing at us."

Violet herself laughed at those remarks.

"Mr. Howland," Thane said, "I don't see them smirking or laughing. When I look at Elizabeth's son, he's usually in tears."

"For the benefit of the jury," Jonah said.

"Your Honor," Paul began again.

"Mr. Howland," Thane said, "you chose to prosecute that young man's mother for three murders. Did you expect him to come into this courtroom to observe her trial and not become emotional? During much of his mother's testimony, he isn't the only person in this courtroom in tears. Now, Mr. Howland, do you have any evidence linking Ms. Sutherland or her client to what happened on those television newscasts last night? If you don't, I'll deny your motion. I can't concern myself with the news media. Those reporters have a First Amendment right to say whatever they want about jury nullification. I don't care who Ms. Foster or Mr. Neumeyer went to law school with."

"Even if there is no link," Jonah said, "the People are entitled to a mistrial. You know as well as I do, those jurors know all about jury nullification now. Everybody in this courtroom was talking about it this morning."

"Your Honor," Paul began one more time.

"Mr. Howland," Thane said, "this is a court of law. I don't know what the jurors know about jury nullification or anything else. Do you have any evidence that they've willfully disobeyed my order? That they've watched, heard or read news reports about this trial?"

Jonah sneered. "Will you let me question them about what they know?"

Thane threw up his hands. "Mr. Howland, how can I do such a thing? I can't let you ask these jurors what they know about jury nullification. I'd cause a mistrial if I permitted any lawyer in this case to mention jury nullification. And that includes you. I'm denying your motion."

*****

Gideon had laid down the usual rules for the twelve jurors and the two alternates the day they were selected. They were not to read newspaper articles, view television newscasts or listen to radio news reports concerning the trial of Elizabeth Daleiden. Nor were they to discuss the case in any manner with any other person, not even a spouse or a child.

He'd done that in lieu of granting Tanner's motion to sequester the jurors in a hotel in Oxford, order the county to pay for their room and board, and direct the sheriff to make certain they had no access to any form of the media or participated in any unmonitored conversations with other persons, not even with members of their families.

"This isn't the Soviet Union, Mr. Howland," Gideon had seen fit to add. "We still call it the land of the free."

*****

"You know," Belle said during the salad course in Thane's dining room, "I've heard those people whispering. I sit right there with them among the spectators. They must be using some kind of code, though. I had no idea they were plotting."

Paul laughed with the others but still came down from the levity with a worried look on his face.

"I have to confess," he said, "I'm rather concerned about your judge. A trial where the court gives the witnesses free rein to tell the jury whatever they wish is most unusual, to say the least."

Jonah and Violet put their salad forks down and stared at Paul.

"Don't get me wrong," Paul said. "He's as much my hero as he is yours. If your state's attorney loses his case, as I pray to God he does, of course he can't appeal, but he can file a complaint against the judge with the Judicial Inquiry Board. Do you suppose Judge Heidecker has thought about that?"

"I'm rather certain he has," Jonah replied. "If Tanner Howland loses his triple-murder case against Elizabeth Daleiden, though, I doubt he'll want to keep it in the public eye by filing a complaint against the judge. Other trial judges in the state, Republican and Democrat alike, would rush to Gideon's defense. We'd hear more than we ever wanted to hear about a trial judge's discretion, especially in a murder case. No judge, they'd say, wants to send an innocent person to prison for the rest of her life."

Thane looked at Jonah and nodded his head vigorously.

"I think you're right," he said. "Gideon knows he can get away with what he's doing."

Jonah and Violet picked up their salad forks and resumed eating again.

"I'll be very sorry," Elizabeth said, "if I cause any trouble for Gideon."

"You shouldn't be sorry about that," Belle said. "If anybody should be sorry, it's Tanner Howland. He's the one who chose to prosecute you for murders nobody in their right mind could imagine you'd commit. And he only did it for his own political advantage."

*****

After the meal, Elizabeth, Violet and Belle took their after-dinner drinks to Thane's library. Thane collected original editions of books. But not without reading each of them, he said, "upon purchase." Belle had arranged for his purchase of a number of them.

Thane, Paul, Jonah and Eli took their after-dinner drinks to the living room.

"This is just like the old days," Elizabeth said. "The gentlemen in one room, the ladies in another."

The two deputies parked outside Thane's house would drive home all the guests except Paul, who would stay overnight with Thane. Thane and Paul had served each course with two extra plates, which Eli and Jonah filled and took out to the deputies.

"Damned good food," the deputies agreed.

"Okay, you lawyers," Eli said, after he and the other gentlemen had seated themselves. "Can you explain something for me? Why did Judge Heidecker seem so relieved when my mother told him she saw no signs of a struggle in her father's bedroom?"

Thane and Jonah looked at one another.

"I was holding my breath on that one," Thane said.

"So was I," Jonah said.

Thane turned to Eli. "If your mother had testified that she saw signs of a struggle but she'd lied to the deputies in order to cover for Henry and Titus, she would've admitted she was guilty of aiding and abetting their murder of her father. Tanner would've nailed her to the cross."

Paul also turned to Eli. "That would've been a clear case of aiding and abetting. Violet must've warned your mother."

"Why would my mother need a warning?" Eli asked. "She was simply telling the truth."

Jonah turned to Paul. "I feel certain Violet and Elizabeth discussed the matter at length. They could both probably qualify as experts on aiding and abetting at this point. But I agree with Eli. His mother needed no warning. She was simply telling the truth. Olivia was right. We can all tell the difference between a liar and an honest person."

*****

"We see you on the news every night," Frank's nineteen-year-old friend Mike Hammond said to Eli. "No matter which channel we turn to. They show you and Jonah and your mother going up the courthouse steps, or coming back down, every day. The reporters treat you like royalty. It's so obvious they're on your mother's side. Did you know that?"

Eli looked at Jonah, as if for help, but once again found none.

Eli had happened to answer the telephone when Frank called. Eli thought he and Jonah should attend the party just to show Frank they didn't hold a grudge against him. Jonah agreed to go, but not without saying it wouldn't be the first mistake he'd made.

A deputy who was younger than Jonah had driven him and Eli to Chicago. He sat on the first-floor deck, where he could keep an eye on both of them. Frank had served him a plate of appetizers and a pitcher of lemonade

Frank had also promised Jonah and Eli he wouldn't light a joint in the deputy's presence.

"We don't have much time for watching ourselves on television," Eli chose to tell Mike.

Jonah smiled. Eli had told Mike the truth.

"Did you know," Mike's boyfriend Tom Cutler asked Eli, "you guys were doing it in the same bedroom where your mother's gay friends murdered her father?"

"Okay, that's enough," Frank said.

He pointed with his drink at the two nineteen-year-olds sitting opposite him in the circle of five lawn chairs in the garden behind Jonah's two-flat. It was early in the evening of the second Saturday in August.

"You guys promised me," Frank continued, "you wouldn't ask Eli and Jonah questions like that. Now you either shut the fuck up and behave yourselves, or I'll kick your asses out of here."

Mike and Tom laughed.

Wearing shorts that fit them snugly despite their slender bodies, they sat with their mostly bare legs spread as far apart as the arm supports of their chairs would allow.

"Wouldn't Jonah be the one," Mike asked, "to decide who should leave and who should stay? I thought this was his backyard garden."

But it was Frank's party, Jonah wanted to respond. Then he thought better of it.

Tom turned to Eli.

"Your mom encouraged you guys to have sex?"

This time Eli didn't try for help from Jonah.

"My mother knew we were both gay. She could tell we liked one another. She encouraged us to do what she could see we wanted to do. Why wouldn't she?"

Those remarks surprised Mike and Tom.

"Our parents never encouraged us," Mike said.

"They think we're living in Chicago because the women here are easier to lay than those virgins they've got out there in Iowa," Tom said. "They'd die if they knew we were gay."

"Have they seen your landlord on television," Jonah asked, "going up and down the courthouse steps with Eli and his mother?"

"Oh, yeah," Mike said. "They know you're our landlord. We had to tell them that."

Tom looked at Jonah. "Is that really the bedroom you and Eli do it in? The one they talk about on the news?"

"Oh, come on, guys," Frank said. "I warned you. Keep your mouths shut about that."

Mike ignored Frank. "I'd like to be in on a struggle in that bedroom," he said.

"So would I," Tom agreed. "With the guys who sleep in it now— and do whatever else they do in it."

Jonah was relieved to know he needn't worry any longer that Frank might take undue advantage of his nineteen-year-old tenants.

Chapter Twenty-Seven

On Monday, August 15, Violet resumed questioning Elizabeth.

"You testified last week that you were thirteen years old when Henry and Titus explained to you they were men we'd now call gay."

"Yes, I was thirteen when they told me that."

"In their explanation, they told you they weren't brothers, they didn't have the same last name, and the man known as Titus Hassenauer was in fact Titus Peltz?"

"Yes, that's what they told me."

"Did you hear Thane Sorenson testify in this trial that you were also thirteen years old when Henry and Titus decided to leave their farm to you?"

"Yes, all those things happened at the same time, when I was thirteen."

"Did you hear Thane Sorenson testify that Henry and Titus had a lawyer change the land trust documents under which they owned their farm?"

"Yes, they made me a beneficiary of the trust along with them. I became a co-owner of their property. If anything happened to them, I'd be the sole owner."

"And they told you what they'd done?"

"Oh, yes. They even gave me a copy of the trust agreement with the bank in Chicago. They told me to hide it somewhere and keep it safe. I'd have it to prove I was the owner when the time came for me to do that."

"How do you remember you were thirteen when these things happened?"

"The war had just ended. It was 1945. We'd dropped those bombs on Japan. The people who'd fought in the war, and survived it, were coming home. The day after Labor Day I'd start eighth grade."

*****

"You've already testified, Elizabeth, you listened to every word of Olivia Daleiden's testimony in this trial. I want to read part of what she said about Henry and Titus. First, Mr. Howland asked her: 'Why would the neighbors want to kill the old men?' Olivia replied: 'Because they were homosexuals. For years, those men had lived on that farm posing as brothers. Then it turned out, shortly before they died, they weren't brothers. They'd lied when they said the younger one, Titus, had the same last name as Henry. The story went around that Henry and Titus were men who enjoyed other men the way God wants men to enjoy women, and only women.' Is it true, Elizabeth, the neighbors found out, shortly before Henry and Titus died, they weren't brothers but were what we'd now call gay?"

"Yes, that's what happened."

"Do you know how that happened?"

"Yes, I do. Two Sundays before Henry and Titus died, Olivia came to see Daniel. As soon as she showed up that afternoon, I left the house to do some outside work. At that time, Olivia wanted Daniel to quit farming. She was pushing him to apply for a job she'd heard was open at the bank in Oxford. If Daniel didn't want to go into banking, she thought he should at least think about teaching in high school somewhere."

Elizabeth had her eyes fixed on Olivia.

"Daniel and I were twenty-three years old then. We'd both earned bachelor's degrees at Northern. It was difficult commuting to and from classes in DeKalb, working our farm and doing most of the work on Henry and Titus's farm as well, but we did it. Olivia and Daniel's father didn't pay a dime for Daniel's tuition or other expenses either, nor did he ask them to. Daniel always tried to tell his mother we attended college not to become bankers, lawyers or doctors, but just to be educated people. Olivia didn't have any use for that kind of talk."

"And I still don't," Olivia said from her front-row seat. "Look where your education has brought you, Elizabeth. You're on trial for three murders. And you should be on trial for four."

"That ought to get her thrown out," Jill whispered.

But it didn't.

Gideon turned to Elizabeth.

"Please continue your testimony," he said.

"Olivia also told Daniel he was wasting his time helping Henry and Titus with their work. She said at the rate Daniel was going, he'd always be poor. My farm was only one hundred sixty acres. Where would a farm that size get him when we started raising children? Daniel thought he had to listen to Olivia because she was his mother, but those remarks made him angry. He told her Henry and Titus had done almost all the work on my father's farm after my mother died and I was still too young to be much help. Daniel told his mother it was only right that he and I should do the work we did for Henry and Titus now that they were too elderly and ill to do it themselves."

Elizabeth shook her head as if she still couldn't believe what happened next.

"Olivia wouldn't listen to anything Daniel said that day. She told him he had no obligation to help Henry and Titus just because he was married to me. Then Daniel tried to prove to Olivia our helping Henry and Titus made more sense than she realized. He got out the copy of their land trust agreement with the bank in Chicago. He showed her I was a co-owner of their farm. When they died, I'd be the sole owner. We'd have the income from three hundred twenty acres to support any children we had. We'd have no debts to pay. What more could we ask?"

Elizabeth wiped her eyes with her handkerchief.

"Take your time," Gideon said, almost whispering.

"Unfortunately," Elizabeth continued, "the lawyers and the bank used Titus's real last name in that document. And Olivia saw it. 'Those two old men must be queer,' she told Daniel, 'just as I thought.' He pleaded with her not to tell anyone else what she'd seen. But she refused to promise him she wouldn't. That same day she started telling people about what she called the 'scandalous situation' involving Henry and Titus and the 'queer-lover' Daniel had thoughtlessly married."

Olivia chose to interrupt Elizabeth's testimony again.

"You've always been a queer-lover, Elizabeth. You still are. You let a queer have his way with your own son, my grandson. And look at that lawyer of yours. You want people to believe she and that woman she lives with are straight? Straight to hell, I'd say."

Gideon motioned to the deputies.

"Take her out," he said. "And don't let her back."

In the commotion that followed those orders, Tanner stared forward with his elbows on the counsel table and his hands on either side of his head like blinders. He couldn't bring himself to watch the deputies escort his chief witness out of the courtroom.

Just before Olivia reached the main door to the courtroom

behind the spectators, she turned and glared at Eli, Jonah and Belle.

"The judge orders a God-fearing woman out," she yelled, "and lets those queers stay."

*****

As soon as the deputies resolved the matter of Olivia's outbursts, Gideon once again told Elizabeth she could resume her testimony.

"Daniel was extremely upset that he'd inadvertently exposed Henry and Titus. He went to them in tears and apologized. But they didn't want him, of all people, feeling bad. They called him their 'son-in-law from heaven.' So they made a joke about what he'd done. They said it was time people learned the truth anyway. When I was alone with them, though, I could tell they were devastated. They couldn't face being thought of as men who were homosexual, not after spending their lives denying it, even telling people they were brothers so they'd have a reason for living together."

Elizabeth wiped her eyes with her handkerchief again.

"Do you need a recess, Elizabeth?" Gideon asked.

Elizabeth shook her head. "That won't be necessary. I've already taken up too much of your time."

"No, Elizabeth, you certainly haven't done that."

"I don't want to be unfair to Olivia," Elizabeth said. "She did one good thing I'll never forget. Shortly after Daniel and I started living together, the war in Korea began. I remember the date. It was June 25, 1950, one month to the day after Henry and Titus murdered my father. Daniel could've been drafted. He also could've asked for a deferment because he was attending college. He refused to do that, though. If he got drafted, he said, he'd go over there and fight. He didn't believe he should be able to get out of the war just because he could afford to go to college. That's another thing Olivia didn't care for at all. We found out later she came up here to the Selective Service office in Oxford and got the form for Daniel to claim the student deferment. I suppose she had a right to do that. He was still a minor, and she was his mother. Anyway, she filled out the form, forged Daniel's signature on it, and sent it back."

Tanner rose to his feet. "Your Honor," he said.

"Please sit down, Mr. Howland," Gideon said. "You heard what I let your chief witness say in this courtroom. Now I intend to hear what Elizabeth has to tell us about Daniel and Korea. I know you served in that war yourself. Please sit down."

Tanner sat down.

"Daniel and I didn't know what Olivia had done until the war in Korea was over. She'd given the Selective Service office her address as Daniel's address. They'd sent all his papers to her. I may seem selfish about this. I know other young men and women, including Mr. Howland, served in that war. And many of them were injured, and some of them died. But if I'd known what Olivia was doing, I would've helped her. I would've at least made no attempt to stop her. She kept Daniel home and safe, and for that I have always been grateful to her from the bottom of my heart."

"My God," Jill whispered.

Elizabeth turned to Violet. "I'm ready for your next question."

*****

"Were you present in this courtroom when Clyde Lewis gave his testimony regarding the deaths of Henry Hassenauer and Titus Peltz on December 17, 1955?"

"Yes, I was."

"Do you recall him giving his opinion that Henry and Titus must've been dead before the fire started?"

"I heard him say that."

"Do you know whether or not his opinion was correct?"

"I do know. Clyde Lewis was an astute observer."

Elizabeth paused, looking at Eli and Jonah.

"Henry and Titus were dead," she continued, "before the fire started."

"How do you know that?" Violet asked.

"I was in their house with them," Elizabeth said, "when they died."

Gideon once again knew he could only let the tumult in his courtroom exhaust itself like the wail of a petulant child. He once again called a brief recess in the trial and left the bench.

Chapter Twenty-Eight

As soon as the uproar subsided, Gideon returned and sat down.

"Ms. Sutherland," he said, "you may continue."

"Did you hear Clyde Lewis testify that another deputy sheriff found an empty rat poison container in the garbage pail in Henry and Titus's kitchen?"

"Yes."

"Did that in fact happen?"

"Yes."

"Did Clyde Lewis confront you with the rat poison container?"

"Yes, he did."

"What did he say to you?"

"He asked me if I put the poison in the food I prepared for Henry and Titus that day."

"What did you say to Mr. Lewis?"

"I told him I'd never do such a thing."

"Did Mr. Lewis pursue the matter with you?"

"No, he didn't."

"Do you know why the empty rat poison container was in the garbage pail in the kitchen?"

"Yes, I do."

"Why was it there?"

Elizabeth wiped her eyes.

"Titus," she said, "put it there."

Hearing those words, Jonah realized the enormity of the mistake he'd made. The mob hadn't killed Henry and Titus—even as it had.

*****

"Do you know what Titus did with the poison?" Violet asked.

Elizabeth struggled vainly against her tears.

Gideon motioned to the court reporter that he was going off the record.

"Elizabeth," he said, "I can stop this right now."

"I know you can," Elizabeth said. "Violet told me you can. But please don't do that. I need to finish my story. I need to complete my day in court. Please let the jury decide whether I'm telling the truth or not."

"My God," Jill whispered again.

Gideon turned to the court reporter.

"We'll go back on the record."

Elizabeth turned to Violet.

"I know what Titus did with the poison," she said. "I watched him do it."

"What did he do with it?"

"He put it in a large Mason jar of the hard apple cider he and Henry made every autumn. They often drank a glass or two of it before they went to bed. That afternoon they drank the whole jar."

*****

Elizabeth looked at the jury she'd "reduced to tears," as the reporters would say and write that evening.

"I didn't want to see Henry and Titus do that. Even before word got around that they weren't brothers, they'd mentioned to me they were thinking it might be best, as they said, to 'bring things to an end.' Henry was eighty-five then. Titus was seventy-five. They were both sickly, Henry especially so. Titus could still take care of Henry, but he didn't know how much longer he'd be able to do it. I could see that was a legitimate concern. Daniel and I offered to care for both of them as long as they needed us. We guaranteed them they'd die at home. We'd sacrifice farmwork if we had to."

Elizabeth turned to Gideon. "Do I need a question from my lawyer here? I seem to be rambling. I'm sorry, Your Honor."

Gideon looked at Elizabeth and shook his head.

"You aren't rambling," he said. "You don't need a question. You may continue."

Jonah wondered if a state's attorney had ever filed a complaint against a judge for presiding in the case of a murder defendant he was secretly in love with.

"After the news got out that Henry and Titus weren't brothers, they made up their minds. They said they could only be a burden to Daniel and me in the future. We couldn't convince them they'd only be an inspiration for us as long as we lived. They said we'd serve them best

192

by letting them go. They'd had a good long life together. They were especially glad they'd shared it with my great-uncle Karl, my mother Emma, and Daniel and me. But enough was enough. Daniel and I should spend our time caring for the children we wanted. They were our future."

Elizabeth glanced at Eli and Jonah and let a smile break through her tears.

Then she turned to the jury again.

"Neither Henry nor Titus wanted to go on living without the other. They thought that was the most important reason for deliberately ending their lives. Daniel and I could never take the place of the other. And especially not in a world that knew they were—"

Elizabeth turned to Gideon.

"May I use the word they used?"

"You may," Gideon said.

"In a world that knew they were 'queer.'"

Tanner had a hand to his forehead as if he were shielding his eyes from an oppressively bright light.

Elizabeth continued. "I refused to help Henry and Titus with the poisoned cider. They said they'd read enough in the books Titus got from the library here in Oxford to know they couldn't let me assist them. I admit, though, I stayed with them all through their ordeal. When they vomited, I held a pail for them. I cleaned it off their faces. They were in horrible pain at the end. They went into convulsions. Finally, they couldn't breathe. I held their hands. I told them over and over how much I loved them. Then I watched them die. First Henry. Then Titus."

*****

"I brought this on myself," Elizabeth said to the jury. "Henry and Titus didn't intend for me to be present when they took their lives. They planned to do it by themselves. They knew it would be gruesome. When Daniel and I looked in on them later that night or the next morning, we'd find them dead and call the sheriff. They thought the deputies would notice the empty rat poison container lying on top of their other garbage and assume two old men exposed as homosexuals had killed themselves. If the coroner wanted to waste the county's money on autopsies, his people would find the strychnine in their blood. Henry and Titus never imagined I'd be accused of assisting their suicides, let alone murdering them."

Elizabeth shook her head.

"But I insisted on being with them until the end. I actually hoped I could keep them from taking the poison. I didn't understand how much they wished to be done with the struggle of living. Titus especially didn't want to be alone, without Henry. What could I say? They'd lived together fifty-seven years. Olivia's exposing them as homosexuals was the last straw."

In the overwhelming silence that followed those remarks, Elizabeth turned to Violet.

"What caused the fire?" Violet asked.

"That was also my fault," Elizabeth replied, turning to the jury again. "I wasn't thinking clearly that day. When I was certain both Henry and Titus were no longer alive, I left their house. I planned to go back later that night with Daniel, find them dead and use their telephone to call the sheriff. I'd kept the fire in their fireplace going all the while I was with them. I should've put it out before I left their house, but I couldn't bring myself to do it. Even though I knew they could no longer feel anything, I couldn't leave them in a cold house. It didn't seem right."

Elizabeth shook her head again.

"I paid the price for that decision. The fire must've spit an ember onto the floor. And Titus was no longer able to stomp it out before it caused any real damage. When Daniel and I saw their house was on fire, we could only start the call chain for the volunteers and run over and try to stop the blaze ourselves. When the neighbors showed up and made their hateful remarks for people like Jonah and his grandmother to hear, I realized things had changed. Everybody would believe, as Jonah did, a mob had set the fire. So, unless the authorities wanted to create an ungodly uproar, they'd have to say the fire started accidentally. And that's what they did."

"Did Daniel know the truth?"

"Oh, yes," Elizabeth replied. "After the fire started, I had to tell Daniel the truth. He would've blamed himself if he thought the neighbors killed Henry and Titus."

"Did you ever consider telling the authorities the truth?" Violet asked. "Did you ever consider telling them you were present while Henry and Titus committed suicide, and the fire was what they said it was, an accident?"

"Yes, initially I did want to do that. I was the one person who knew for a fact the people in the crowd, despite their stupid talk they never should've assaulted the ears of a six-year-old child with, didn't kill Henry and Titus or set their house on fire."

"Why didn't you tell the deputies the truth?"

"Daniel and I decided I couldn't," she said. "As soon as I told him the truth, he was adamant I could never tell anybody else. He pointed out, correctly, that after the neighbors learned Henry and Titus weren't brothers, we came under suspicion ourselves. We'd obviously known all along they had different last names. Daniel was very afraid that if I revealed I was present in their house when they committed suicide, I'd be prosecuted for assisting them. We agreed we had no obligation to disclose what actually happened the day Henry and Titus died. Instead, we'd let people choose whichever version they wanted. Either a hateful crowd killed them, or they died in an unfortunate accident."

Elizabeth looked at Eli.

"We never even told our son the truth. We had no desire to bring the innocence of his boyhood to an end with that awful story. When he was old enough to hear the rumors and asked us about it, we simply told him the authorities said it was an accident. Other people told him it was anything but an accident. I believe he decided the matter was too painful for us to speak of. And it was. So he dropped it, for our sakes."

Elizabeth turned to Jonah.

"Then Jonah Neumeyer came back to Revere. He's been right all along. I couldn't admit I'd failed to protect the two men who'd protected me."

Jonah stared at Elizabeth. The mob hadn't killed Henry and Titus—and yet it had.

"Jonah thinks his return to Revere brought me to this courtroom and put me on trial for three murders. But he has nothing to apologize for. He couldn't anticipate Olivia's outrageous hoax, that hospital conversation she made up, as Violet says, from beginning to end."

"Elizabeth," Violet asked, "were you and Olivia ever alone in Daniel's hospital room last Christmas Day?"

"No, her second visit to the hospital room never happened. But I'm actually grateful she told that lie. I hope she's never prosecuted for it. She forced me to finally tell the whole truth about everything. Not just about the deaths of Henry and Titus, but my father's as well."

Elizabeth turned to the jurors one last time.

"And that's why I'm sitting here today telling you this dreadful story. My problem has always been wanting to believe people are basically good. I detest cynicism, and yet I often can't help but think the cynics must be right, and I'm wrong. If you choose to convict me of crimes I didn't commit, I'll forgive you. We live in a confusing world."

She turned to Gideon.

"I have nothing more to say."

*****

Gideon turned to Violet.

"I have no further questions for Elizabeth," Violet said

Gideon looked at Tanner. "You may cross-examine Elizabeth."

Tanner shook his head. "I have no questions for Elizabeth."

"You waive your right to cross-examine the defendant?"

"I do."

Chapter Twenty-Nine

On Tuesday, August 16, Elizabeth, Eli, Jonah, Belle and the two deputies came to court with an elderly man. He took the arms Elizabeth and Eli offered to help him make his way up the courthouse stairs.

Belle and Jonah climbed the steps ahead of them and behind the deputy in the lead.

"Who is he?" Jill asked Jonah.

"You'll soon find out," Jonah replied.

"Why is he here?" one of Jill's competitors asked Elizabeth.

Other reporters loudly demanded to know the stranger's identity.

The man between Elizabeth and Eli paused when he reached the top of the stairs.

"I'm a witness in Elizabeth Daleiden's trial," he said to the reporters in a surprisingly strong voice. "I have testimony to give. The judge and jury need to know what I have to tell them."

Inside the courtroom he took a seat in the front row of spectators between Eli and Jonah. Others moved to accommodate him. After Gideon ordered Olivia out of the courtroom the previous day, there was extra space in the row.

Violet called Albert Gartner as her next witness.

Eli helped him all the way to the chair Elizabeth had most recently occupied.

"Thank you, Eli," Gideon said.

*****

"How old are you?" Violet asked Albert.

"I'm ninety-three."

"Where do you live?"

"I live in Fort Lauderdale, Florida."

"Do you live there by yourself?"

"No. I live with my grandson and his boyfriend. They take care of me. They put me on the plane to Chicago last night. They encouraged me to come back here."

"Come back here?" Gideon asked. "You used to live here?"

"I lived the first eighty-five years of my life in Revere. My wife and I owned the hardware store in Revere."

"Gartner Hardware?" Gideon asked.

"That's what we called it."

"You put a sign up for me when I ran for judge."

"Yes, we did," Albert replied. "I remember that."

Gideon looked at Tanner. "Mr. Howland, do you see a conflict?"

"No, Your Honor," Tanner replied, remaining seated. "They put up signs for me, too."

"Yes, we did," Albert said.

Gideon turned to Violet. "You may continue."

"How long did you own Gartner Hardware?" she asked.

"Sixty-three years. My wife and I bought it from her father and mother when we were twenty-two. They let us pay the purchase price in twenty annual installments. My wife died of a heart attack when she was seventy-six. We had three children and eleven grandchildren, but none of them lives around here anymore. Even I couldn't resist my grandson's invitation to live with him and his friend in Florida when I retired eight years ago. I don't live the life they do, but I enjoy lunches and cocktail parties with their friends. They'll never get me to one of their disco bars, though. I'll dance with them at home but not out in public. That's where I draw the line."

Albert had let Jonah, still in his teens, use his grandmother's checks, with only her signature on them, when he bought hardware items for their farm. Jonah would fill in the date and amount of the check. Albert would use his Gartner Hardware stamp on the "pay to the order of" line.

"Did you keep the financial records for Gartner Hardware?" Violet asked.

"Yes, I did."

"Do you still have any of those records?"

"Yes, I do. All of them. My grandson helped me take them down to Florida. We put them in storage."

"What do those records consist of?"

"Mainly, two notebooks for each year Gartner Hardware was in existence. That's one hundred twenty-six notebooks."

"If I looked in those notebooks, what would I find?"

"If you looked in an expenditures book for a year, you'd find a daily record of everything we paid out, whether in cash or by check. To suppliers and employees mostly. The taxes we had to pay are in those books, too. In a receipts book for a year, you'd find a daily record of every sale we made to a customer. A few refunds, too, from suppliers for defective items we sent back to them."

"A daily record of every sale you ever made?" Gideon asked.

"Yes, Your Honor. In my own handwriting."

"What would you write down for every sale you made?"

"The name of the customer, the item or items the customer bought and the total amount of the sale."

"For every sale, to every customer?"

"Yes."

Gideon turned to Violet again. "You may continue."

"Did you call the defendant, Elizabeth Daleiden, ten days ago, on Saturday, August 6?"

"Yes, I did."

"Why did you call her?"

"I realized I had evidence to give in this trial."

"How did you come to that realization?"

"This case is in the news down there. My grandson and his friend saw it on television. They asked me about it. I told them I knew Elizabeth and Daniel. Henry and Titus, too. When Jonah and Eli let everybody know they were gay, I told my grandson and his friend I knew them as well, when they were boys. But what really did it for me is when that deputy sheriff started talking about the rat poison."

"Mr. Gartner," Violet asked, "did your store sell rat poison?"

"We were the only store in Revere that sold it. The drugstore and grocery store didn't want to carry it. They sent people looking for it to us."

"And you're here to tell us about one such sale in December of 1955, are you not?"

"Yes, I am. On December 16, to be precise. It surprised me at the time. That must be why I've remembered it so well. People like Elizabeth and Daniel, Emma and Karl, Jonah and his grandparents, and Henry and Titus didn't buy rat poison. They didn't need to. They always kept at least one cow, even after they gave up dairy farming and started raising hogs. Every day, they put some of the milk in a pan for the cats that lived in their barns. Those were domestic cats, but they lived wild.

You couldn't pet them. You didn't dare let young children near them. But they killed and ate rats and mice. Those people knew that. That's why they fed the cats enough milk to keep them around but not enough to keep them from killing every rat and mouse they came across. Those people had no need to buy rat poison from us. They let nature take its course, they said. They had no use for any poison on their farms."

"But one of those people did buy rat poison from you on December 16, 1955?" Gideon asked.

"Yes. Violet has the notebook titled '1955 Receipts' in front of her. I brought it with me from Florida. It's open to the page where I recorded a sale of rat poison on that date. When I made the sale, I asked what the problem was. I was told the cats were no longer doing their job. I had my doubts about that. I knew Elizabeth and Daniel were awfully fastidious in running both their farm and the farm Henry and Titus owned. They probably could've kept the rat and mouse populations down to a manageable level without having the cats around to help them do it."

Gideon looked at Albert. "Who bought the rat poison on December 16, 1955, the day before Henry and Titus died?"

"Henry couldn't drive anymore, but Titus could, at least the two miles to Revere and back during daylight."

"Who bought the rat poison?" Gideon insisted.

"Titus. I put down Titus Hassenauer in my notebook even though I'd heard that wasn't his real last name, and he and Henry weren't brothers. I still wanted to be respectful."

"Elizabeth Daleiden never bought rat poison from your store?"

"Never. Titus was the only one in their group who did. And just that one time, the day before his and Henry's house burned down in that awful fire. I was there. I saw Elizabeth and Daniel. I saw Jonah and his grandmother. I heard what the loudmouths in the crowd were saying. I don't blame Jonah for assuming the worst. I did. And I was the one who sold Titus the rat poison and might've been able to see the truth—if I'd allowed myself to imagine those two old boys wanted to take their own lives. I knew they were both ailing. In any event, Elizabeth is innocent. Titus bought the rat poison. That's why I came here to testify."

"Thank you, Mr. Gartner," Gideon said, making no attempt to hide his tears. "Thank you for coming all the way from Florida to testify in my court in this case."

"You're most welcome, Judge. I thought it was the only thing I could do."

*****

Tanner waived his right to cross-examine Albert.

"The defendant has nothing further to add," Violet said.

"Evidence in rebuttal, Mr. Howland?" Gideon asked.

"I have no evidence in rebuttal," Tanner replied.

"Closing argument?"

Without rising from his chair, Tanner looked at the jurors.

"The defendant has had her day in court. So have the People. Now you have to decide whether or not Elizabeth Daleiden has told you the truth on the three charges the People brought against her. I trust you'll make the right decisions."

"That concludes your closing argument?" Gideon asked.

"Yes," Tanner replied.

Gideon turned to Violet. "Ms. Sutherland, your closing argument?"

Violet, also without rising from her chair, turned to the jury.

"The defendant, Elizabeth Daleiden, believes the evidence speaks for itself. She also trusts you'll make the right decisions in this case. She doesn't see any need for her lawyer to tell you what to think."

*****

During Gideon's instructions to the jury, Jonah noticed some activity among the jurors. The one in the middle of the first row who'd taken notes throughout the trial handed her neighbor on her left her tablet and ballpoint pen. The neighbor read the top page of the tablet, appeared to sign it and passed the tablet and pen to her neighbor on her left.

Gideon's instructions included an unusual number of examples of activities associated with crimes that didn't constitute aiding and abetting. Without question, failing or refusing to report the crimes of others—and "becoming a snitch," he said—wasn't, by itself, a crime.

Well before he completed his instructions, the middle juror in the front row had regained possession of her tablet and pen from the juror on her right.

When Gideon informed the jurors it was time for them to retire to the jury room, select a foreman, deliberate the case and reach a verdict on each of the three counts of murder, the middle juror in the front row rose to her feet.

"Your Honor, may I speak on behalf of the jury?" she asked.

Jonah knew Gideon had also seen the tablet and pen of the middle juror in the front row circulating among her fellow jurors and their alternates.

"Yes, you may," Gideon replied.

"Each of us has signed a statement," she said.

"What does the statement say?" Gideon asked.

The middle juror in the first row held up her tablet and read from it.

"'We the jury believe the defendant, Elizabeth Daleiden, is innocent of all three charges against her. We believe any further deliberation on our part would be pointless and unnecessarily prolong the fear among Elizabeth and her loved ones that a confused or hateful jury might find her guilty.'"

*****

"We'll do it this way," Gideon said. "Every juror and alternate juror who believes Elizabeth Daleiden is not guilty of the charge of murdering Jacob Reifert on May 25, 1950, please raise your right hand."

All the jurors and alternates immediately raised their right hands.

They did so two more times after Gideon substituted Henry Hassenauer and then Titus Peltz for Jacob Reifert and changed the date to December 17, 1955.

Chapter Thirty

After the conclusion of Elizabeth's trial but before their final meeting with the reporters on the courthouse steps, Violet took Eli to Gideon's office behind his courtroom. Gideon readily accepted Eli's invitation to the dinner party he and Jonah planned for Elizabeth that evening.

Violet, Belle, Thane, Paul and Albert also came to celebrate.

Elizabeth and Gideon sat side by side on the couch in the living room and at the table in the dining room as if they were on a date.

*****

Within a week, Sheriff Darrell Glendenning agreed with Elizabeth, Eli and Jonah. They no longer needed the protection of his deputies, although they would miss their company.

*****

One Saturday in September Gideon came to Elizabeth's house for supper and later accepted her invitation to stay overnight.

"What do you think about that?" Jonah asked Eli.

They were in their bedroom with the door closed.

"Mom deserves to have another man in her life," Eli replied. "And I'll be damned glad if Gideon is the man. Don't you agree?"

"I couldn't agree more."

"They're going to have to keep it a secret, though."

"What?" Jonah asked. "Why do you think they'll need to do that?"

"He was the judge at her trial. He can't be dating her."

"He sure as hell can. The trial is over. If they'd been dating during the trial, it would've raised all sorts of questions. But not now. They're free to do whatever they please."

"Are you sure about that?"

"Why don't you ask Violet or Thane?"

"Won't they charge me for their legal advice?"

"What makes you think I won't charge you for mine?"

"I'm spending my extra cash on my education. I can only pay for your advice with sex."

Down to his undershorts, Jonah gave Eli, who was already naked, a hug.

"What makes you think," he asked, "I want money?"

*****

Despite the collapse of his triple-murder case against Elizabeth, Concord County State's Attorney Tanner Howland refused to give up his dream of becoming a congressman.

Warren Glendenning, his opponent in the Republican primary, had stood so close to Elizabeth during her last interview with the media on the courthouse steps that she turned to him laughing and asked if he wished to make a comment.

"Warren is the grandson of the sheriff who refused to pursue me for murders I didn't commit," she explained to the reporters. "For some reason, he's attended every moment of my trial. I've heard he intends to run for Congress next year against Tanner Howland."

Warren threw his arm around Elizabeth's shoulders and praised the jurors for refusing to waste everybody's time by deliberating in "a badly misguided prosecution of an obviously innocent person."

He chose the day after Elizabeth's acquittal to declare his candidacy for Congress. His campaign literature featured pictures of him hugging Elizabeth on the courthouse steps. In the Republican primary election on March 21, 1978, he defeated the Concord County state's attorney he called "odious" by a margin the media deemed "humiliating."

Howland, the reporters liked to add, was the state's attorney who'd prosecuted Elizabeth Daleiden, the woman who'd farmed a half-section of land for many years, for three murders she didn't commit. They no longer referred to her as "the farmer's widow."

*****

Tanner and Warren agreed on one thing: Warren never had a supporter in Tanner's office who surreptitiously delivered a copy of Olivia's statement to Violet.

"Maybe the court reporter did it," Belle said.

She and Violet were taking their seats at their dining room table with their Saturday evening guests: Elizabeth, Gideon, Eli and Jonah.

Elizabeth turned to Violet. "Do you remember the court reporter's name?"

"Charlene Tillich," Violet replied.

Elizabeth laughed. "She told me she'd become a court reporter. She did it after her three children all grew up and left their farm."

"You know her?" Eli asked.

The other four persons at the table stared at Elizabeth. They wanted to learn the answer to Eli's question as much as he did.

"Oh, yes," Elizabeth replied. "Tillich is her married name. She came to the hospital to see Daniel last Christmas Day. She's good about coming to the reunions, too. She was in our class in grade school and high school. She knew your mom and dad, Jonah. She's one person who speaks of them kindly."

*****

Later that spring Jonah sold his two-flat in Chicago to Frank, Mike and Tom. Although Frank provided all the money and creditworthiness for the deal, he insisted it was only right that Mike and Tom be joint owners of the property with him.

He'd not only broken down the defenses of his younger friends. He and they were now in a "ménage à trois," as he told the amused closing officer, who happened to be gay.

That hardly meant, though, Frank and his friends were exclusive.

"When we get you and Eli on board," Mike told Jonah in a private moment after the closing, "we'll have the five-way of our dreams. Do you know what they call such a thing in French?"

"I'm sorry," Jonah confessed, "I have no idea. Maybe you should ask Frank about that."

*****

Jonah used most of the proceeds from the sale of his Lincoln Park two-flat to pay Elizabeth half the appraised value of her farm. Jonah's money was more than sufficient for her to pay off all her debts.

Elizabeth, Jonah and Eli thereafter owned the farm jointly.

Elizabeth chose to live in Oxford, though, with her new husband, the Honorable Gideon Heidecker.

Another judge in the Oxford courthouse officiated at their marriage ceremony in his chambers. Eli and Jonah were their only witnesses.

*****

A few days later, Jonah was picking strawberries when he saw Olivia driving her black Buick toward him. She parked on the shoulder and rolled down her window.

He was working so close to the road she had no need to step out of her car.

"I understand that slut Elizabeth has married Judge Heidecker," she said.

Jonah chose not to respond.

"I'd say that's all the proof I'll ever need."

"Proof of fucking what?" Jonah asked, without interrupting his work.

"Isn't it obvious—even to you? If a judge who wasn't biased in Elizabeth's favor had presided at her trial, she'd be in prison right now, where she belongs."

Jonah once again remained silent.

Eli was taking his last final exam. He, Elizabeth and Jonah planned to start baling the first crop of hay the next morning.

"I've always known how clever that woman is," Olivia said. "She tells the jury her two dearest friends murdered her father. Why not? They're no longer around to deny they'd ever do such a thing. I used to see those old fairies shopping in Revere. They couldn't kill a flea if they tried. And she convinced that silly one, Titus, they had rats and he needed to buy some poison to kill them. So he goes to town and buys the rat poison she uses to murder him and that other old queer. Clever, clever, clever. And all those phony tears she shed on the witness stand. She must've had a slice of raw onion in her hankie."

Jonah continued his work as if he'd heard nothing more than the summer breeze.

"I'm selling my house in Revere," Olivia said. "I've arranged to spend the remainder of my life in a convent. I've written a will leaving all my money to the Catholic Church. Although if I had any grandchildren, I'd leave it to them."

"You don't consider Eli your grandson?"

Olivia scoffed. "Heavens no. He can't possibly be related to me. I'm certain that wretched boy is the result of his whore mother sleeping with a man who wasn't my precious Daniel. Eli will probably never know who his real father is."

Jonah stood up and briefly considered smearing Olivia's face with the strawberries in his basket. Then he realized such a stunt could only end in his disappointment that the red ooze wasn't her blood.

"After Elizabeth killed Daniel," Olivia continued, "the only family I've had is the church—the strict church that insists murderers like Elizabeth and sodomites like you and Eli will spend eternity in hell."

Jonah laughed. "I'm not really worried about it."

"You should be very worried about it. So should Eli. I like what Anita Bryant is doing down in Florida. She knows what evil sinners you queers are."

And with that, Olivia, laughing herself, drove off.

And, Jonah hoped, out of his life forever.

*****

On a Saturday afternoon in June, Eli and Jonah hosted a party on the lawn east of Karl's path to celebrate Elizabeth and Gideon's marriage. For dessert, the hosts served strawberries and Eli's homemade ice cream.

The other lawyers present—Gideon, Violet, Thane and Paul—said they found it difficult to believe Jonah would rather be a farmer than a lawyer.

"I don't find it difficult to believe at all," Belle said.

"Neither do I," Elizabeth said.

Darrell Glendenning and Charlene Tillich agreed with Belle and Elizabeth."

"He also intends to write," Eli said.

"How nice," the juror from the middle of the first row said, "a literary farmer."

"What do you intend to write?" Belle asked. "Fiction?"

"Maybe someday I'll graduate to that," Jonah replied.

Belle wrote lesbian romance novels under a pen name, but nobody in Concord County was supposed to know it. In her latest book, though, her main character had an eighteen-year-old brother, Eddy, who had a twenty-eight-year-old boyfriend, John. In a subplot, John's hedonistic, cynical but alluring ex, Hank, did everything he could to entice Eddy into his world.

"Jonah's already finished his first book," Eli said. "I'm helping him edit it. And it isn't fiction."

"Can I hope to feature it in the store someday?" Belle asked.

Jonah laughed. "If I publish it, I'll need signed waivers from all of you."

"Why would you need waivers from us?" Violet asked.

The other lawyers echoed her inquiry.

"I'm not a lawyer," Eli said, "but I think the title of his book will answer your question."

"What's the title of your book, Jonah?" Elizabeth asked.

Jonah assumed he appeared as guilty to her as he did the morning after he first slept with Eli—which was in his book. But he replied anyway.

"Elizabeth Daleiden on Trial."

Author's Note

If you enjoyed this novel, please consider leaving a review at the website of the bookstore where you bought it.

I will also be grateful if you leave a review at https://www.goodreads.com.

Ron Fritsch

www.ingramcontent.com/pod-product-compliance
Lightning Source LLC
Chambersburg PA
CBHW060042150626
46556CB00018BA/2490